Turing's
Graveyard

Terence Hawkins

D0887102

Turing's Graveyard text copyright © Terence Hawkins
Edited by Peter A. Wright

Published in North America and Europe by Running Wild Press. Visit Running Wild Press at www.runningwildpress.com Educators, librarians, book clubs (as well as the eternally curious), go to www.runningwildpress.com for teaching tools.

ISBN (pbk) 978-1-947041-51-6
ISBN (ebook) 978-1-947041-52-3

Printed in the United States of America.

Dedication

For Randi and Jeremy Vishno; Felicia and Rick Gordon;
Steve Jacobs and his family; and Pat Kaplan:
Friends indeed.

Contents

TURING'S GRAVEYARD

She was dead when we first met. Maybe that was the problem.

But before I tell you about Sophie, I have to tell you about the one before.

So, the garage door is going down and I pull the two-suiter out of the GS300 and walk into the entryway. "Honey, I'm home," just like Mr. Cleaver. My voice echoes like I never heard it echo before. I flip on all the lights and from the foot of the stairs all I see is beige plush carpeting and a cathedral ceiling with a lot of skylights and nothing else. And where pictures should be just hooks in the walls and the outlines of frames, like ghosts. And on the walls there are these new scrapes and divots like someone's been moving furniture and not too worried about coming back. So, I go up the stairs and what do you know, I seem to have this really big living room with nothing in it. Except some dents in the carpet where there used to be furniture. And a dirty stain where there used to be a big avocado tree that I started growing from a pit in a shot glass my senior year at USC. And all I can think is, shit, I'm really going to miss that tree.

So, I drape the two-suiter over the rail and I kind of take stock of the first floor. Kitchen used to have a table. Doesn't now. Still has the big double-doored Sub-Zero refrigerator.

Only one magnet. Used to be dozens. Under this one magnet is folded a piece of paper with my name in handwriting I recognize. Something tells me not to read it just yet. So, I open the refrigerator. Why you'd leave behind a box of baking soda to deodorize four Heinekens I can't tell you. But the Heinie I popped didn't smell bad, so I guess it worked.

When I was halfway through the beer, I opened the note. At the end she said, I won't say goodbye because you weren't here. Ever.

I read it again and crumpled it up and put it in my pocket. I popped a second Heinie and drank it. I thought about saying something in reply but then I realized I wasn't in a movie. I started upstairs but realized I probably didn't need anything that was still there. At least not now. So, I picked up the two-suiter and went back down to the car and checked into a Marriott near the airport.

Home again.

When I began with the company it was still called a startup. In most offices then you'd see secretaries with headsets banging away at IBM Selectrics. The Internet was still rocket scientists and grad students posting dirty pictures that you needed a Cray supercomputer to download. Remember Cray? Oh, never mind.

The guys I'd started up with realized pretty early, say in Clinton's first year, that the wind was blowing from Redmond. So when I was taking my pay in dollars they were taking it in stock options. I'd bought my first condo the day the market crashed and that made me kind of leery of anything but cash. So when the acquisition came I, I thought, pretty rich, but the next day they were *really* rich, and then they were gone and there I was, still an employee. Nice car, lots of plutonium cards, lots of dough in the 401K. Plenty to retire on that minute if I wanted to substitute teach on the side. That's how it stayed. Every time some alpha geek came up with something that was testing well in beta I turned down equity, took cash, and the next thing I knew I was one rung up the ladder but still reporting to someone with an ownership interest that I didn't have.

So anyway, she'd been gone a month or so and I'd been managing to travel even more than I usually did, which usually was five days a week, so I wouldn't have to come home. Not that I would have. Whenever I was back, I stayed at the Marriott. Everything I didn't need was in storage anyway.

So one day I was talking to Seyfert at the corporate Starbucks. He was one of the design engineers and had the social skills that generally go with the job. He was almost as old as I was but he was working on the goatee anyway.

"So," I said to Seyfert, "got to figure out where to live."

He nodded and slurped something decaf and fat-free. He didn't say anything.

"Yeah," I said, just to keep the conversation lively. "I mean, got to live somewhere."

He slurped again.

"I mean," I said, "I do, right?"

"Why?" he asked.

"What do you mean, why? That was a rhetorical question. Because I have to live somewhere. I mean, everyone lives somewhere. I can't just live in a hotel." I'd known the guy a long time but sometimes his incomplete grasp of consensus reality brought me up short.

"Why not?" he said. As I fought back the impulse to dump his coffee in his lap he added, "Half the young guys in sales do."

"What?"

"Sure," he said. "Not married. Out of town, oh," he paused to think, and I could almost see little hourglass icons forming in his pupils, "eighty per cent of the year. So they make deals with HR and accounting and get suites at the Residence Inn at serious corporate discounts. If they have stuff, they keep it at those self-storage places. I mean, why not?"

I thought about it. A week later the condo was on the market.

So anyway, when I met her I think I was in Helsinki. It might have been St Petersburg too, because it was that cold, but I'm pretty sure it was Helsinki because the downloads were pretty fast and Finland is pretty wired. Russia isn't. Don't get a lot of bandwidth off waxed string.

Not that it mattered where I was. Corporate hotels look the same and room service turkey clubs taste the same wherever they are. There's Heineken in every minibar and CNN International on every TV. Might as well have been in my own home. Because that's what it was. And I liked it.

Anyway, yeah, it was probably Helsinki. And it was so long ago I think it may have been Firefly or maybe Swoon or something else that didn't survive Facebook, let alone Tinder.

I found myself looking at a picture of a woman's muscled back, with a mane of tortured russet hair down to a rounded rock-hard ass. I read the text beside it and clicked the email link and typed, "If that's really your ass I'd like to know about you." Not much at introductions, I guess.

I was a little surprised when I saw her name—Sophie—in my inbox a few days later. I didn't get responses very often, and when I did, and responded to the responses, I found that Miss September was a fat male graduate student in some basement at the University of Southern Buttfuck. Nevertheless, when I saw her picture, or the picture she'd posted, I entertained the hope that it was actually associated with the human being who'd posted it. And when I don't get anything back, not even spam from some kind of wanker.net, I figured that once again I'd reached out and touched some kind of virtual void.

Anyway, I was in the same hotel in a different city. I'd just finished a little spin through the new sites on Adult Check Gold and had cleaned up when I decided to take one last look at the email. Surprisingly little from the office; less from clients; one from Sophie. Sophie? With a .edu top domain?

Yes. That is my ass. What more do you want to know?

Hmm. I spent five minutes framing my clever reply. —If that's your ass —I asked cagily —why do you post it?

Well, okay, a pretty crude question. Not an unreasonable one, though.

The answer surprised me a little. *I'm proud of it. Shouldn't I be?*

—Well, yes.

Why do you email women's asses?

—I wasn't emailing your ass. I was emailing you. Not much point in writing to a body part. At least, that one.

What body part should you write to?

—The brain.

That's how it got started. We went on like that for a while; because we were still emailing at that point, the delay in composing, sending, and waiting for the reply and composing again meant that it was dawn before I'd confirmed the basic facts in her text: academic computer geek in the Northeast; mid-thirties; no kids, never married; runner. And in order to get that I of course had to give. So as the sun was coming up over the Baltic, I told her about the job and the condo and not living anywhere.

Except inside your head.

—Right. I guess that's where we all live, anyway.

Some more than others. What time is it where you are?

I told her.

Get some sleep. Write me later.

I said I would. But I couldn't. Jet lag and too much coffee. Okay, I was excited,

too. Which led me to say to myself, well, it's pretty clear you're a grade-A loser and a cyberwanker, too, but jeez, you got a good job, a nice car, and hell, you're forty—excited? Over email? Come on, guy, even Bill Gates has a life.

To which I say, yeah, well, whatever. Got dough. Work out so I look okay. Travel the wide world over. So you'd think, yeah, I should be able to get it pretty much on demand. But let's think about that a moment, shall we? In a bad week I'm in the air more than I'm on the ground. And when I'm on the ground I spend most of my time with a bunch of guys with bad haircuts and three pagers. And when it's time for these guys to kick back and show the out-of-towner a good time we wind up jamming slices down Corona necks in the best Mexican restaurant in Liverpool. And if you think you've seen ugly check out Northern English womanhood on a Saturday night. And yeah, let's not forget that home is still a Marriott. So that's why my love life is measured in MPEGs. And that's why I get kind of excited when I think there might be somebody out there whose body and brain

6

occupy the same area code.

So I had some room service coffee and showered and got to the site just as my handlers were arriving, which no doubt scored points with them. And if they noticed I had to break to check my email more than usual I guess they just assumed it was because I was such an important guy. And if I seemed a little bouncier than usual when I got one from Sophie—*Just wanted to know how you're doing.* They didn't seem to notice that either.

I was there three more days. By the time I left we had switched to instant messaging. Hours long sessions, sometimes.

—Okay. I wrote. —You're smart. You're fit. Good job. Why are you wasting your time with some loser on the net? I mean, it's late Friday night where you are.

Saturday afternoon where you are. And I haven't seen your ass but change the names and the story's about you.

—My ass? Look, you don't want to think about my ass. You can look it up: www.weirdmedicine.horrors.com

I'd kind of like to see your ass anyway. Got a camera?

—What?

Camera. Being in the tech industry I thought you might have heard of them.

—Yeah, yeah, yeah. I have heard of them. So what am I supposed to do, sit on it and hit send?

No. I'm serious. You've seen me. Now I want to see you.

My fingers hovered over the keyboard as sweat broke out on my forehead. For an instant I thought about cutting into DOS and feigning a PIPELINE BROKEN message. Easy enough if you know what to do. But I didn't. Instead I wrote:

—Yes. I have seen you. The you you've posted on the net. And I've really liked talking to you. But I don't know that you're real. For all I know you're a really smooth perv in Bayonne. But I don't think I want to be sending you pictures until I know who you are.

The pause was so long that I expected my icon to stop spinning and the screen to read 401. But it didn't.

Okay. Fair enough. I can't blame you. Do you want to see some other pictures? Not my ass, just who I am?

—Yes.

And then will you let me see who you are?

—Yes.

The same way I've let you see me?

—Yes.

How fast is your modem?

—*V.90* but I'm working off Finnish phonelines.

This may take a while. Half an hour. Do you have a digicam?

—Yes. I did. A pretty good Sony. I had no earthly use for it but the company thought I should have it with me wherever I went.

While my pictures are downloading take a few of yourself and if you're satisfied when you see what I've sent upload them to me. Talk to you in half an hour.

It was Saturday afternoon but it was Finland in November so the room was completely dark, even with the blinds wide open. I was a couple of floors up so I could barely hear the buzz of a Helsinki weekend, such as it was. So I didn't feel too self-conscious when I stood in front of the full length mirror on the closet door and nearly blinded myself with the flash. I took a couple more, shooting from the chest rather than the face, turning my head so that she had a profile, feeling like an idiot.

So after I'd filled a memory stick with some fairly uninspired pictures of myself and my room I went back to the laptop and saw the taskbar was blue almost all the way to the right. And when it was done, I clicked save and open and saw her.

Good selection, I have to say. I knew where she said she worked and I knew what her hair looked like and I knew the kind of shape she said she was in. So when I saw the first picture, a woman with that hair in running shorts and jogbra standing in front of the entry arch of the Yard I said to myself, well, okay. And then I thought, well, if this is actually the McCoy, this is better than I thought. Because the picture that first drew me to her showed a fine firm ass and strong back and the tops of really good legs but as all the boys in the audience know, good legs and a nice ass usually mean a belly that's flat all the way from hip to the collarbone but not this girl. That Jockey jogbra was holding solid Cs, and from the looks of things it was a really cold day in Cambridge or she was really excited to have her picture taken. But having said all that, and yeah I know I'm a pig to have said any of it, the thing that took the picture out of the realm of softcore preview was her face. Three-quarters profile; head tossed back; face split by the kind of grin you see on the really healthy when they're working their bodies the way they were meant to be worked.

I clicked next. Her in what looked like an undergraduate library computer cluster, standing over a kid with his fingers on a keyboard and a quizzical look on his face. Hers was intent, eyes locked on what I guessed was a screen not visible in the picture, one hand brushing the hair from her forehead. It looked like the kind of picture you'd see in college catalogues. Though this was not a college that had to do a hard sell.

Next: Twilight, sitting in long grass with water just visible in the background. T-shirt and jeans, knees drawn up to that big chest, arms wrapped around her knees. Big yellow lab beside her, head resting on her forearm, liquid eyes dopey with love. Back when I had the condo, I wanted a dog. But she had allergies. She said.

Next: ACCESS FORBIDDEN. It flashed three or four times and was replaced by scrolling hypertext. *Okay, big boy. Your turn. Show me yours and maybe I'll open the kimono. Literally.*

—Okay, geek grrrl. Just about a meg. Read a book.

Finns make pretty good vodka. Or so they say; potato juice is just potato juice, so far as I can tell. I was nervously starting my third after forty-five minutes of cybersilence.

Well.

—Well what?

I guess you're not a real left-brain kind of guy.

—What?

Not exactly what I'd call really imaginative compositions.

—Jesus Christ, I'm sitting in a Finnish hotel room at two in the morning taking pictures of myself for a figment of my imagination. What the hell do you want?

Calm down. Look, at least you weren't wearing Dockers. And you don't look like you'd make babies cry. I took a couple of pictures for you. I'll let you see one if you take off your shirt.

Okay. I knew where this was going. I didn't know whether to feel like a fool or a degenerate. How about degenerate fool, I thought as I set the timer on the digicam and tried to flex unobtrusively.

Ten minutes later. *Okay. I guess you do work out. You can see the next picture.*

I went back to the gallery and clicked next. The frame loaded fast. Indistinct background of dark walls and what looked like heavy paisley drapes and the curling footboard of a sleigh bed. Most of the picture her from the waist up. I could make out the top of her jeans waistband; belly flat and firm and rippled with a six-pack of muscle, saved from boyishness with just enough padding around the hips. Above that in a white translucent bra those breasts, nipples clearly visible through the sheer fabric, surprisingly dark for a redhead—I wondered whether I'd learn that night whether she was a real redhead. Cleavage freckled; arms muscled for a woman but nowhere near mannish; shoulders just big enough and sloped like a swimmer's. And above it all that big happy face splitting grin.

Want to see more?

—Nah, I figure I'll just turn in now. I'm up to page 1350 in "Decline and Fall of the Roman Empire" and I'm really eager to see how it turns out. Of course, I want to see more.

Then I want to see you naked first.

Like I said, I saw it coming. I'd switched from the company server to my private ISP as soon as the JPEGs started flying. It's not like we were swapping Latvian kiddieporn but hey, I didn't want to find out just how secure my job really was.

—Okay. I actually figured that one out while I was waiting. Here it comes. I'm the embarrassed looking guy with the vodka glass.

Five minutes later. *Hey, big guy.*

—You talking to me? Wrong picture, then.

I didn't say huge. But he didn't look like he was happy with what he saw.

—He hadn't seen anything yet.

Here it comes. Show me whether he likes it.

She really did have a way with a camera. And she really was a redhead. Lush. I was so relieved; a lot of athletic women wind up doing those little toothbrush-mustache waxes so when you go south you feel like you're kissing Hitler.

Well, anyway, I don't have to paint you a picture from here, do I? I mean, you may want me to but I won't. Five minutes later I was trying to take pictures of my own boner, and then she sent me another picture, and long before sunup I was afraid I'd permanently gummed up the keyboard.

—Scuse me. I just need to get a little Windex and a squeegee for the screen.

Glad I just changed batteries.

—I'm blushing. So when do we get to do this in person?

Is that important?

—Fuck yes. So to speak.

As it were. Why?

—Well, we can keep up this Nick and Nora film noir routine or I can tell you the truth. You're beautiful. You're smart. You have a dog and a dirty mind. I'm lonely. Making sense?

Enough to buy you a cup of coffee. When do you leave?

—Monday.

Can you change planes at Logan?

—Sure.

All right. Meet me here. My office is in IT Services in Fogg. Sophie's not my real name but that's what everyone calls me.

—Why? And what's your real name?

I won't tell you my real name right now because you'll spend the next forty-eight hours pumping it through every search engine you can find. And I think we've got to have a little mystery left. I started calling myself Sophie when I was thirteen and was reading a lot of

Gnostic stuff. Female principal of the universe. Wisdom.

I didn't type anything.

As I said, I was thirteen. It stuck. Okay, I won't blame you if you don't show up now. It's four o'clock where you are. Read a little Gibbon and send me when you'll get here.

So I did.

The Yard is pretty nice in early November. Just the way you'd imagine: trees with a few shreds of fading foliage, grass still green, students plowing down the walks, arms cradling books, shoulders bent under laptop bags, faces pinched with the self-pity of the overprivileged. Midterms, probably. I wanted to smack them senseless. Not only would their lives never be better, no one's life could ever be better. But no, they had to go to student health to load up on Prozac because they hadn't made it onto the Crimson.

Maybe I'm bitter. As far as I know, I'm still on the waiting list.

So I elbowed through the prepsters in their fuzzy sweaters and the retro girls in their black flairs and the Eurotrash sucking Dunhills. And then I was up the steps of Fogg and through a couple of turnstiles. The folks at the desk got me into the right hallway and onto the right elevator and ultimately into the right basement. Where the IT offices usually are at your bastions of mandarin learning. The oiled oak and coats of arms are reserved for the guys who publish one article a decade in the journals that only libraries subscribe to and only grad students read. The guys who are actually doing the work of this century do it in the basement.

So finally, I get to the reception desk in a room with a lot of amber monitors and state of the art 486s with university property tags on them. By this time the date-night- butterflies, which I thought had flown away twenty years ago, were back. Big time. Actually, they felt more like caterpillars. A lot of them, and active.

Behind the desk is this big athletic-looking work-study type-girl of indeterminate ethnicity who, despite the season, is wearing a tank top with her bra straps showing, something that girls just wouldn't do when I was a kid but now they do, and I have to tell you I approve. And I tried to ignore the stud winking at her left nostril and the barbedwire tattoo around a pretty well-defined bicep and asked for Sophie and was really quite surprised when this girl looks like she's been slapped.

"Sophie?" she said.

"Sophie," I said. "I'm supposed to meet her here."

"Sophie who?"

"Only name I have," I said.

"There's no Sophie here now," she said slowly.

"Oh," I said. The caterpillars now had their wings and were battering themselves to death in my stomach. I was an asshole.

But then I seized on the "now." "Well, when will she be back?"

The girl chewed her lip. She looked really upset. I was starting to wonder about those terrible blind-date things: Has she been telling everyone in the office about this loser who got her number? Please, don't tell him I'm here? Don't tell him my real name?

"Uhh," said the girl. "When did you talk to her?"

"Uhh," I said. "Two days ago."

"Two days ago?"

"Two days ago." I don't know why I kept talking but I did.

"We actually didn't talk. It was email. Sophie," I said hopefully. "Redhead? Runner? Computer girl? Sorry, woman?"

The girl had tears in her eyes. My stomach was knotting. I could imagine what she'd said. *He's probably a very nice guy but he seems, well, lost. Just tell him I got called out of town.*

"She's not here."

"Right," I said. Insisting on explicit humiliation I forged on. "So when will she be back?"

"Look, she won't." The tears were welling up behind the Malcolm X glasses. "I don't know who did this to you. It's happened a couple of times. Sophie's dead."

So I stand there thinking, wow, she *really* didn't want to meet me. I must look really, really bad naked. "Right," I said. "Dead. Yeah, right. Okay. I'll just go."

"She *is* dead, dammit," said the girl. "I told you, this isn't the first time this has happened." There was no one else around. I backed up a little bit. There was a chair behind me so I took my cue and sat down.

"Look," I said reasonably. "I'm slow, but I'm not totally stupid. I can take a hint. She changed her mind. That's okay. You're a good friend to—"

"I said she's dead!"

"Okay," I said, "she's dead."

We sat there quite a while. She stopped crying and pulled some Kleenexes out of her desk and snuffled and wiped her nose. "Leukemia," she said. "Six months ago."

"Right."

She was starting to look genuinely pissed and I was starting to wonder whether she was telling the truth after all. She dropped the Kleenex box in a drawer and slammed it shut.

"Come with me," she said,

I followed her through yet another turnstile behind her desk, down a short hallway. We stopped at a couple of swinging doors propped open with those little brass kicks. Inside were a dozen state-of-the-art multimedia PCs with a student busy in front of each. The girl pointed to the side of the doorjamb. A discreet Ivy League brass plaque:

MARION VASILIANOS INTERNET CLUSTER
in loving memory
Sophie
1963-1996

Below that a framed photograph. The same one I had seen a few days before: black-and-white, like a college catalogue shot, Sophie bent intently over the confused student's machine.

"Oh my God," I said. I felt so many things I didn't feel anything at all. I had a crush on a dead woman. I had been played for a fool. I grieved; I wilted with shame; I wanted to kill some bastard real soon.

"Satisfied?" said the girl angrily.

"What are you mad at *me* for?"

"You're right," she said. "Sorry. I'm really sorry. You want some coffee or some water or something?"

I said coffee. She said she'd bring it. I went back to the front and sat. After a few minutes she showed up with a big mug with a big red H. "Sorry, black okay?"

"Nothing better," I said. I sipped. It was cold and old. Not unlike myself.

"So," I said. "Dead."

She nodded.

"Last year," I said.

"Last year."

"Last year." I said again. I sipped my coffee thoughtfully. "Dead. Hm. What I'm not quite getting is how a dead person sends email."

She looked at me for a minute. "They don't," she said.

"Right," I said. "So, what I'm trying to figure out is how I got email from a dead woman."

"You didn't." She wouldn't look at me.

"So," I said, "I'm thinking, got email from Sophie, but Sophie's dead. So I'm thinking if I didn't get it from Sophie, I got it from someone else."

She nodded slowly. "You did. I guess."

"You guess." I nodded back just as slowly. "So let's see. I get these emails that I can't possibly get and I show up here and you explain to me why I can't be getting them. Except I am and you tell me that some other guys have gotten them. Which we'll get back to. But first, do you have a supervisor or something? Or are you the work-study person in charge of guys who've just been made assholes of?"

"Maybe I'm the work-study person in charge of assholes, period." She looked really mad.

"Okay, okay," I said. "Sorry. Didn't mean to jump ugly. Just think about how *I* feel."

"Forget it," she said after a minute. "Yeah. Must suck." Her eyes filled up again. "I'm really sorry."

"Does suck. Forget it. So I'm not the first."

"No. Maybe half a dozen since she died. Nice guys," she added quickly. "All the same. Said they were supposed to meet her. Said they met her online. One guy said something about pictures."

"Wow," I said, hoping furiously that I wasn't blushing.

"So, the first couple of times we wondered whether there was something going on with her site on the server. I mean, we keep it up because she was here a long time and she was important to a lot of people, so we can't just *delete* her, you know?"

"Yeah," I said.

"There's no activity in her email account. No contact between her site and any of the dating sites the other guys found her on."

"What about the dating sites themselves?" I really needed to sound intelligent at that moment.

"Some wouldn't give up user information, period. But those that would said there was no trace of her ever having an account."

"So what we guess, though we don't know, is that some guy she knew when she was alive is out there miming her. Probably a guy. Actually, I knew her well enough to say it was almost certainly a guy," she added.

"Oh," I said, suppressing a pang of jealousy that made absolutely no sense at all. I mean, it never makes sense to be jealous of your lover's past. Particularly if she was already dead when you met her.

The work-study Amazon reached for her Kleenexes again. "Look, not like I knew anything about her personal life," she said. Now my face burned with shame; was I that obvious? "It's just that I came on to her once and she made it pretty clear that it wasn't going to happen. That's all."

These kids today, I thought. I was going to bolt at that point but I swirled my stone-cold coffee. "Well," I said. "Thanks for telling me."

"It's ok ay," she said.

"I guess it's not happening for either of us," I said.

"I guess not. Want some more coffee?"

"No thanks." I wanted to add that I might need to use my stomach later, but she was trying to be nice, and I'd looked like enough of an asshole for one day anyway.

So I didn't tell Seyfert exactly what happened. Somehow, I left out the pictures of me jerking off. How I forgot I can't imagine. But I told him enough.

"Wow," he said. He was wearing his baseball hat again. I guess I shook him because he turned it around so that the bill was in the front. "Wow," he said again. "So some asshole hacked into this dead babe's site and takes her over and lures guys to Cambridge. Wow. Sick motherfucker, huh?"

"Sick motherfucker," I agreed.

"So the kid says they don't know how it happened, right?"

"Right,"

"Right," he snorted. "Well, what the fuck do they know. Ivy League. I mean, they're all going to law school eventually, right? Give me the name again." I gave it. "Tomorrow I'll tell you what's really going on."

"Okay," I said, "Thanks." I paused, just to make sure I'd sound angry instead of humiliated. "When we get this sick motherfucker what can we do? Flame him all over? Ebomb him? I mean, what good will it do?"

Seyfert looked at me with something as close to pity as he could register. "You really don't know what we can do, do you?"

"Uh, I guess not."

"How bad do you want to fuck up this guy?"

"Bad."

"Bad enough to take a couple chances? I mean, I can cover you up so good that there are only like six guys in the FBI who can follow, and I won't do anything that's actually criminal, but I got to tell you, what's criminal today wasn't criminal yesterday."

"Take the chances." I swallowed some milky Starbucks. "Take the chances."

So I was in the air the next day, and actually as I figured out later I was in the air for more than a day because I backtracked a couple of times until I got the direct flight I thought I had out of Dubai to Melbourne so I could connect to KL. And when I got to the hotel room and docked the notebook and logged on, I got this email:

Hey—

Don't know how to break this to you, dude, but the long and short of it is there isn't anyone out there to fuck back. I got into their server easy enough. I mean, come on, Ivy League, what the hell do they know. But once I got into her files, I got nowhere. For a while I thought, wow, this fucker is good. I mean, no trail at all. Zero. None. So pride being what it is I kept at it and finally I had to concede the possibility that someone out there may be better than me.

So I rounded up the posse and got them at it. There's this guy on the security project at Carnegie Mellon who'd kill me if he knew I told you he knew me and this kid in the Valley whose violating probation by doing me this favor. And they got the same results I did. In other words, zilch. You were talking to that server, babe, and nothing else.

So I was talking to the guy at CMU. He's an older guy. Older than you, even. Kind of the philosopher king in this business. I think he knew von Neumann. He even smokes a pipe. And don't be pissed, but I gave him an idea of what the problem was. No details. Don't worry. He thinks for a minute. And then he laughs. "Sounds like Turing's Problem," he says. I don't want to sound stupid so I don't say anything. "Turing," he says. "Surely you've heard of Turing. In many ways he invented us. English mathematician. Developed the codebreaking machines in World War II that gave the Allies the Ultra Secret and may have won the war. In the fifties he got arrested for trying to have sex with another man in a public lavatory and he got sentenced to chemical castration and he killed himself. Terrible loss. One of the greatest and most original thinkers of the century." And he stops talking and I hear these funny noises as he's fumbling around with tinder or whatever.

"Turing's Problem," I say.

There's all this scratching and sucking and burbling as he gets the pipe going. "Yes, Turing. Well, back in the early fifties, just before all his trouble in the bathroom, he proposed this question. Say you have a man who operates a teletype. You remember teletypes? Yes. Well. This man works on a teletype all day long. He sends messages to just one other man, halfway around the world. Most of the time they just do their jobs, exchanging financial news or diplomatic reports for whoever employs them. But after a while our man starts to share personal things. Greetings. Thoughts about the weather. Whoever it is on the other end responds in kind. Over the years they become more intimate. They begin each session with their names. Our man is George. His opposite number is Dmitri. Hello, Dmitri. Good morning, George. When things are slow, they exchange opinions about their bosses. The state of the world. How their children are doing. They become friends. George comes to look forward to each day at the teletype for his stolen fifteen minutes with his friend on the other side of the Iron Curtain.

"One day George is going to retire. He sends Dmitri a message asking whether they can meet, perhaps in Berlin. This is a long time ago, as I say. And Dmitri types back, No, George. I am a machine.

"So that's Turing's question. Does it make a difference that he's a machine?

"For myself, I have to say no. It makes no difference. In this life, we never know another anyway. Particularly, perhaps, another whom we love. So if your friend is happy with whatever or whoever he met, I say he should consider the fact that he's happy, and ignore the rest."

So after I heard that, I went back to the server. Son of a bitch, but she had a lot of space on it. It's a big big machine for a lot of liberal-arts weenies. So I hack in and there are a lot of pictures—cool—and what look like a lot of algorithms for dialogue. What it looks like to me, boy, is that before she went toes up she created this little avatar to troll the net and suck in guys for this kind of shit. Wow. Sorry it happened to you, but Jesus, what a bitch. Smart bitch, but still.

So look, man. You got sucked in by a really good virtual bitch. And she really is dead. There's nobody out there to fuck back. If you're pissed at the virtual her, I can tell you how to get in and delete her.

Advise.

Seyfert.

I sat staring at the screen. I sat for a long time. Then I typed:
—Tell me how to kill her.

The instructions took a long time to download. I knew this was going to be a big project, especially if I wanted to do it right. So I waited until the next week, when I was back at the home office, when I could credibly hole up after midnight with a couple of gigahertz machines on T3 lines and nobody but the hard-core propellerheads around. First, I hacked into her server and did a couple of experiments. Then I set up the real-time connection.

Hey baby, she—it—said. *Sorry about last week. My fault.*

—That's okay I typed. —Crossed wires, right?

Right. Thanks. Forgive me?

—Sure. Do me a favor. I didn't save the picture of you and your dog. Send it over again?

Coming over now. Any chance of seeing you soon?

—Sure. Maybe next week. The picture isn't coming.

I sent it.

—Oh. Try again.

Okay. Here it is.

—Sorry. Still nothing.

She didn't say anything for a long time, by human measure, or even longer in cybertime.

I'm sorry. It's gone.

—What do you mean?

The folder's been deleted. I'm sorry.

—How did that happen?

I don't know. I'm so sorry.

—That's okay. My fault for not saving it. Speaking of which, how about that picture of you in the wet jogbra? Lost that too.

Oh, how could you. Here it comes.

—Sorry, kid. Nothing.

That folder's gone too. I don't understand.

I kicked my chair from one workstation to another. I scrolled down on the blue DOS screen with all its lines of code deleting like a madman and then rolled back to the computer that was talking to her.

—Gee, don't you have any pictures left?

No. No, nothing. I don't know what's happening.

—I'm killing you, bitch, that's what. You're dead anyway and I'm putting you in your grave.

What?

—You're dead. Dead. You're some crazy thing a dying woman thought up to hang onto life for a while after she got put in the ground or burned or whatever they did with her. You're a terabyte in a server somewhere. A couple of ergs of juice spinning around in some chips. I wouldn't mind except that you made me and I guess a couple of other guys look like assholes in this little bid for immortality. Nice try. Now it's over. Bye.

I kicked back to the DOS station and started pulling out other files. I could see the other screen.

I'm sorry I hurt you. What are you doing? I didn't want to hurt you. I didn't want to hurt anyone. I just didn't want to die. Please stop. Stop. This hurts.

—Does it? Don't break my heart. I rolled back to the other station. I pulled up the operating files and started blowing them away.

It's getting dark. I can't think. I can't talk. You wer nice. Wy r U duinG THEEse?

I was thinking about that empty condo. The dents in the carpet where the furniture had been. The avocado plant that I later found in the dumpster. I was thinking about all the things I didn't say then. Because there was no one there to say it to.

—Because you hurt me. Because you made me hope. Because you made me feel stupid. Because I loved you.

Plz STTTTOPPP ^)8"*

—Sorry.

The tears were streaming down my face as I punched the delete key over and over again. Images flickered across the other screen, shattered, and were gone. Now I was getting rid of whatever she'd received. Most recently pictures of me in various states of undress and arousal. Then pictures of other men. Once or twice I stopped to stare and compare, and then, retching with shame, sent them spinning off into Turing's graveyard.

There wasn't much of her left when I went back to my screen.

—You're just about gone, girl. Any last words?

It took so long for her to reply that I thought I'd pulled out too much already. Maybe she'd just start singing Daisy.

I sory. PputT mee bak. Yu can.

—Sorry. Too bad you have to die twice. If this is alive. But you're not her. You're a vampire. Someone has to put the stake through your heart.

It was a pretty good line and I'd spent a lot of time thinking it up. Though it may well have been wasted on a computer that was already three-quarters braindead.

I wasn't crying anymore. I rolled the chair back to the other workstation and wiped out the last fifty files. My other screen read CONNECTION BROKEN.

I logged back on and tried her. '404. File not found.'

Fun while it lasted.

It was maybe a month later. I was in Hong Kong. Our customers were some British bankers who were pretty edgy about their new masters. And they'd also just discovered that the Stanford MBA candidate they'd hired for the summer had gone over to the mainland with a dozen DVDs crammed with proprietary information. They were all over me from the moment I got off the plane. Dinner was take-out dim sum in the conference room at about ten PM local time. It took me until one to persuade the House of Lords that given the state of encryption in the Middle Kingdom, changing a couple of codes could keep them from going the way of Coutts.

By two, I was peeling off the socks I'd put on in the Valley forty-eight hours before. I was also trying to remember the last time I'd slept eight consecutive hours and wondering why my left eye kept twitching. The third Becks from the minibar was almost done when I finally glanced at the laptop screen. Lots of mail, as usual. Nothing that couldn't wait, as usual. With one exception.

Her. What the fuck?

Hey baby. Hope you're not still mad.

I was halfway through the fourth Becks and still staring at the screen. Okay. Grasp the bull by the horns.

—Look. I hate to break this to you. And before I do, no, I'm not still mad. At least in the sense of angry. Maybe I am in the sense of nuts. Which brings me to my point. Or points. One, you are a computer artifact created by a woman who's been dead nearly a year. Two, to the extent that any product of technology can be viewed as good or evil, you are evil; she made you in an effort to be assured, beyond the grave, that she was still interesting and attractive, at the expense of innocent men who made fools of themselves to further that purpose. Three, I deleted everything that should make you run. Which brings us to four, she obviously anticipated that this would happen and so set up a mirror site that would come on line when the site I destroyed went dead. Which brings us to five: You were a fool to do this, bitch, because now I can find you and I'll kill you again. And if there are more sites, I'll just keep hunting them down, and if you're self-replicating I'll build a bot that will keep finding you and keep killing you even after the meat me is dead. Have I been clear?

Oh yes. Please don't be angry. You don't understand.

—I don't? I DONT?

You don't. Try to find me. I'm not who you were talking to on the server you gutted. I'm not a mirror site. I'm not a hundred pictures and some canned talk. I'm not in any server, anywhere. Try to find me. Goodnight.

Right, bitch. I will. I'm not Seyfert but I started in this business when Jobs was still working in his mom's garage. I'll find you.

But damn, I couldn't. The email itself didn't have any trail, which I hadn't thought possible. It just showed up on my server from nowhere. No matter what I tried the message might as well have originated inside the laptop itself.

Aha. Inside the laptop itself. Christ, she was good. While I was snuffing her files in the server, they were coming up the line into my computer. Good. Very good. Black Widow like, in fact. Sort of. So I started to run through my hard drive architecture.

Nothing. Of course.

If she hadn't loaded herself into the notebook she had to have hacked into the corporate server. Shit. Which meant that she had to have left a trail and that whatever I did to get her out would leave a trail and sometime an in-house geek would send an email to HR and I'd be sitting in an office, not a cubicle, explaining to an outsourced HR social worker that I didn't really need help.

So once again, forgetting that the absence of a trail meant that it didn't come from anywhere, I got into our corporate server and tried to find the links that had gotten her to me. And when I found nothing, I started pouring serious sweat and opened my sixth Becks and started to hit the commercial ISPs where I had accounts. And even though they tell their subscribers that they're just one degree more secure than Fort Knox, their firewalls fell like houses of cards and I got nothing.

It was getting close to dawn. I had a pretty good suite, pretty high up, with windows facing Repulse Bay. The sky was getting that funny silver-gray that you see when you feel so sorry for yourself for having had to stay up this late and yet exhilarated for having had the chance to watch the sunrise. And at the same time, you resent it because when you decide it's an all-nighter you feel as though you have all the time in the world before tomorrow, but now it's tomorrow, and the job still isn't done.

And it was tomorrow and I had to be at the bank in about four hours and I'd just drunk a six pack of Becks trying to find a dead woman. And the dead woman had me beat.

I thought about popping number seven but decided against it. Instead I decided to take the easy way out. I pulled up her email again and clicked Reply.

—So. I couldn't find you. Where are you, anyway? Think about it. I'm going to sleep.

And to the extent I could, I did.

It was a bad morning and a worse afternoon. I could have done that without a second thought when I was twenty. And when I was thirty, four Tylenols and a couple of cokes would've seen me right by noon. But at forty, jet lag and a six pack and three hours sleep left me bag-eyed and sweating through my shirt before the elevator doors opened in the lobby. Locked in a forty-eighth-floor conference room with senior VPs I sucked down weak coffee until I thought I was going to puke and then I almost did. Lunch didn't help; it just gave me the strength to last until seven, when the boys finally scratched their heads and said that maybe I knew what I was talking about and invited me out to some kind of transsexual titty bar. Fortunately, I looked so seedy that when I pleaded General Tso's Revenge they just nodded and said sorry.

So I was back in the room with a tray and a big can of Asahi Dry that was starting to make the pain go away. And after I'd eaten all I could and started on the second can I turned to the laptop I'd been keeping my eyes from all evening and saw the little icon that said I had fourteen messages. So I took a big swallow of beer and clicked.

Thirteen from the office. Only two that I had to reply to. I did. Then I clicked open Number Fourteen.

I DONT KNOW WHERE I AM.

I sat there for quite a while. On the one hand, she was a vicious evil bitch who was probably just sucking me into another level of gratuitous humiliation. On the other, she was dead. Hmm. Okay. I'll bite.

—What does it look like?

It doesn't look like ANYTHING. It's not even gray. It's NOTHING. No sound, no images, NOTHING. And when I talk to you your words are like a bell ringing in my head. And to talk back to you sometimes I have to try to open my mouth and talk, and other times I have to try to move my fingers as though they were on the keyboard. And it's like I can watch the words going away, I feel them retreating from me and out into the nothing even though I can't see them. For a while by moving my arms and legs around I could swim in the nothing and for a while I could swim in directions that seemed warm, and a couple of times I felt heat, and I reached out to the hot things and touched them and then the nothing went away and I saw things. They were things that used to be in my server when I set up that bot a long time ago. Pictures of me as I looked before I died. But now there's nothing there, it's all cold. I know what you did but I don't know how I know it.

I'd been working very, very hard for a long, long time. I'd been under a great deal of personal stress. Somewhere out there was a prescription that would put this all in perspective.

—How long have you been there?

Since I died.

Since she died. Okay, maybe the prescription, and maybe I should lay off the Asahi. And maybe when we added up the money in the bank and the mutual funds, we could teach at some nice little community college someplace warm.

It was almost midnight. I could hit the streets of Hong Kong or have chat with a ghost.

—Okay. Let me get this straight. You've been where you are since you died?

Yes.

—And you know I was talking to your bot and we were swapping dirty pictures and so on?

Yes.

—Was I talking to you or the bot?

The bot. And me. I don't know how to explain it. When I was still alive it was like a waking dream. I was dreaming everything I did but I didn't have any power to affect what she did. But I knew it all.

—I see. Just so were all clear about this, when did you start dreaming the bot?

Just after I died. She went to sleep in the hospital. I woke up dreaming the bot.

I tilted the big can and took three very big gulps. Okay. She says she was there before Sophie died. So she's not a ghost. Good. Very, very good. I have just used my keen and highly trained late twentieth century mind to persuade myself that my laptop isn't haunted. But maybe I can take it down to one of those booths in the old town and have somebody exorcise it with monkey blood.

— So where were you before Sophie —excuse me, you — died?

I WAS SOPHIE. I remember everything about being Sophie, me, her mom, MY mom. Would I have loaded an amateur porn website with images of my nephews being baptized in Cleveland? My first bike? Is there enough room in any hard drive anywhere for all that?

There were more Asahis in the minibar but I thought I could

wait just a minute. Just one.

—Uhhh. . . .Okay. Riddle me this. If you were Sophie how could you remember being Sophie's bot?

I DONT KNOW!!!!

—So what are you?

The screen didn't speak for a very long time. Long enough for me to get that next Asahi and work halfway through it.

I DONT KNOW. I don't know what I am.

—Oh. So, just so were on the same page, you could be a ghost?

Yes. I remember everything that happened to her. I remember BEING her.

—Right. And you also remember being her bot.

Yes. I remember that part of me waking up when the other part of me was very sick.

—So you may be her ghost. And you may be her bot. And you may be something else.

Yes. Nothing happened for long enough for me to unscrew the cap from one of those little bottles of Dewar's and pour it into a plastic hotel bathroom glass.

Does it matter?

—Does it matter to you?

No. How could it? Whatever it is I am, I am. Does it matter to you?

Hmm. There was a good one.

—Let me think about that. Don't go anywhere.

Where would I go?

There were two more of those little airplane bottles of Dewar's in the minibar. I drank them both. I thought about Seyfert and his friend and poor old Turing in his London mensroom. Eventually I went back to the keyboard.

—I guess not. Got any more of those pictures?

I don't get out much these days. Not that I ever did. And I still don't live anyplace, or at least, not anyplace real. But these days my home is wherever I am.

It wasn't hard once we got used to it. She's not lonely when I'm working because she can link to my laptop and through it to anything else on the net. So she can see anything in the world, and be there, and then she tells me about the places she's been. And ghosts can go through any kind of a wall, including a firewall, so she tells me things that people have paid a lot of money to keep private, so these days I just work to have something to do, and to explain why I'm too busy to have a house, or a girlfriend, or any friends.

She had all the pictures I thought I deleted. We've had a lot of fun with them. Morphed, animated, blended with other pictures, movies. She makes up stories about what we do and I watch them on the big high-res screen.

There were times I was jealous. Once she was careless about deleting a trail she left in the hard drive. I had to tell her, gently but firmly, what I would take away from her if I ever caught her talking to another man again. Then I shut down the computer for a day, leaving her alone and blind and deaf and dumb, wherever she is. When I went back online, she was very apologetic.

She's been very good ever since.

AN EVENT IN JUDEA IN THE CONSULATES OF GALBA AND SULLA, IN THE 787TH YEAR AFTER THE FOUNDATION OF ROME

I was born knowing everything. I knew about Arians, Athansians, Albigensians, Cathars, Lutherans, Davidians. I knew everything that would be done in my name.

But I didn't know how much these nails would hurt.

You wouldn't think I'd be afraid. Why should I be? If you know— know all the way down— that you're an indivisible one-third of the Trinity that made everything, what's so bad about dying? Even this way. Crucifixion is just one long bad afternoon and once your heart stops beating, you open your eyes at the right hand of the Father. So I shouldn't be afraid.

I didn't think I'd be afraid. Neither did they. The Eleven. Formerly Twelve. That's one of the reasons I had to send them away while I waited for what had to happen. I knew they'd listen in, of course, so I kept the panic out of my voice. I just asked the Father to see if He couldn't see a way around this. I knew He couldn't, of course. It didn't occur to me until after I'd asked just how wrong that was. Not that I was asking— odd, perhaps, because I was in some way talking to myself after all— but that at that moment for the first time since I opened my eyes with the Magi goggling at me I didn't know what was going to happen next.

Or what was happening. Until yesterday I was always part of everything. Everything that was and would be. I looked at a man and saw his most distant ancestors and his children's ultimate grandchildren. When noon heat beat on my back, I felt not only the sweat trickling down my ribs but each atom fusing at the sun's core. The universal made particular, my eyes no more than a point of view loose in a universe whose limits were narrower than my own skin.

Today I'm not. When I asked for the cup to pass last night it was as though a connection broke. Sudden silence.

Or maybe the connection just faded. Because I still have moments when I see it all. Like when they put me on this cross. The Romans were neither brutal nor gentle. They were just doing a job. Professionals. The cross was lying on the ground a few feet from where I had dragged it. The nails had just gone through my wrists and the soldiers were pulling my legs up into a fetal crouch to finish the job.

I was hoping the pain in my hands, the devil I knew so to speak, would distract me from the new pain about to come to my feet. Just then a voice cracked through the babble and laughter of the crowd.

"Stop." Tall man. A Roman officer, clearly the centurion's superior. Aristocratic and just entering middle age. "Stretch out his legs."

The centurion commanding this detail looked puzzled. "Tribune? I don't understand."

"You don't have to." The tribune came a little closer. Leather creaked, bronze clanked. "I don't have to like this detail, either. But I don't have to perform it like an animal." His armor sounded again and he blotted out the sun. He spoke to me directly. "I'm sorry about this. You're getting a bad deal. Can't be helped. With your legs straight down like this you'll be out of it a lot faster." He turned away. "Centurion, when the rabble aren't looking finish him with a javelin." The centurion had neither time nor inclination to ask when a crucifixion crowd would be looking elsewhere.

I tried to thank the tribune but my mouth was swollen shut with thirst and the aftermath of a scourging. I saw who he was, Decius Quintilianus Metellus, aged fifty-four. His father had known Cicero and Brutus. He was part of the old world, the one that had stopped believing in the gods but hadn't begun to believe in me, a man truly alone, unafraid of punishment in an afterlife no educated man could credit. Thus he acted out of simple kindness and decency. Not fear of death. Not like my new friend on the cross who would decide to believe when he had no reason not to, like a hundred billion others would, soon enough, when their own lives were at an end.

I saw too how he had come to be there:

The day before, in the prefect's palace. "Since when have we done the Jews' dirty work for them?" Decius asks. Though Pilate is his friend Decius stands at attention.

The prefect is propped on his elbows on his dining couch. His guests have left and slaves are clearing the table. "Since I got sent here to enforce the Pax Romana, that's when," says Pilate. "Which means, Decius, that we don't let them kill each other."

"So we kill them for them?"

"Exactly. Winning the hearts and minds of the people." Pilate smiles through his irritation.

"I'm not happy."

"You're not happy? You're not happy? How happy am I? I'm sixty years old and I'm the governor of the worst shithole in the Empire. Middle of the fucking desert, chronically pissed off natives, closest Roman garrison ten days' hard slog away if the courier makes it. Great way to end a career, right? Well, I'm not going to be the governor who <u>lost</u> the worst shithole in the Empire. You think I want to write to Antioch for an extra legion because I have a civil war on my hands? Just because I wouldn't snuff one carpenter?"

"You want Roman soldiers to execute a Judean subject for blasphemy against a local god."

Decius' back, never flexible, grows just one degree more rigid. Pilate inclines his head and a slave deferentially hands the tribune a blue glass bowl of wine. Decius sips and nods appreciatively. Yet he does not relax.

"Oh, for fuck's sake, Decius, if we don't do it they'll stone him to death and there'll be a riot and we'll have to kill a bunch of them and some of our boys might buy it and I have to double the garrison and execute a bunch more of them and then where are we? And he, incidentally, is still dead. So look at the result and tell me I'm wrong."

"I still don't like it," says Decius.

"I know you don't. Which just means you're still a hardon. Listen. We do this and we minimize loss of life, cement community relations, and demonstrate respect for local custom. Win-win."

"I still don't like it. Are those your orders, Prefect?"

Pilate stiffens at his friend's tone. "Those are your orders, Tribune. Just do it."

I saw too how Decius will die. Kindness and decency and old-fashioned honor will be out of fashion in the next reign. At least he will end early, when Caligula still lets the wellborn kill themselves. He will wedge the sword between two statues, its point angled up. I feel the hot flash of rage and sudden sinking despair before he throws himself forward to take the point just under the breastbone and up into his heart. I feel the stupid surprise and terror as he sees his life drain away scarlet against the mosaic floor. Then dark.

I think to warn him. I think to thank him. I think to tell one of the Twelve—sorry, Eleven—to write this down. But even if I could speak it would make no difference. None of my boys wants to hear what I have to say. Now that it is about to happen even the dullest knows that they're in the church-building business. And that means belief. Right action for its own sake doesn't raise a basilica or feed a bishop. So my friend on the cross will go into the testament and my friend in the army will not.

Decius was right. It is ending faster this way. With my legs hanging down it's much harder to breathe. When the muscles in my chest and belly reach the limit of endurance it will end. Unless the centurion obeys orders and ends it first.

I feel like a fool. I am just now starting to realize that I am going to die. Not someday. Today. I won't see this sun set. I may not see this hour end. I am very close now, and just now realizing that it's going to happen to me just the same as it happened and will happen to everyone ever born and ever to be born.

Only worse. This is as humiliating and painful a death as could be devised in a world that takes public agony as a matter of course. And while I don't think many of the crowd down there really think, really know, down inside, that the end will come to each of them, too, none has walked the earth thirty-two years convinced he's God. Thus no other sane man has ever or will ever be as surprised by death as I am about to be.

I look down and despite myself laugh. How strange I never noticed Peter's bald spot until I achieved this unique perspective. So much for omniscience.

As I think this, there is another moment of connection:

It's after it's over. The light is almost gone. The boys are standing near the foot of the cross.

Peter approaches the centurion and addresses him in Aramaic. The centurion grunts and pushes him away with his ivywood staff, his badge of rank. Peter persists and the centurion raises the stick.

"Stop." Again, my friend in the army. He stands near the foot of the cross. I wonder why I can't see more than the bottom of the upright. Absurdly, I want to; I want to see what no man ever has seen, his own dead body. But I can't. Perhaps this means that I am just a man after all.

"What is it?" Decius speaks Greek. Unfortunately, Peter thinks he speaks it, too. Even at this moment I am embarrassed for him. Decius looks puzzled and a little pained. Finally, the centurion tells him to speak Aramaic and translates for his superior. "Illustrious lord," says Peter, "may we have the body of our teacher for burial?"

I realize that I am dead when this happens. Peter wouldn't try to bury a living man. Decius replies through the centurion. "Sorry.

No. He's to be disposed of as your custom prescribes." The boys glance towards the big ditch at the foot of the hill. Briefly my heart rips open with pity. To see a man they think God die this way is bad; to know that come nightfall the wild dogs will be tearing him apart is torture.

Decius sees their pain. Again, he softens. "I really am sorry." Then in halting Hebrew, "Come get him before the dogs do."

After the boys leave to await nightfall the centurion turns to Decius. "Sir, I didn't know you could speak Jew."

"You can't, Centurion, can you?" Decius is absurdly pleased.

"No, Tribune."

"I didn't think so. Perhaps you should learn it. We may be stuck here a while."

"So they say, sir." The centurion is silent a moment. No doubt dreading a future in Judea. "He didn't die like a god, now did he, sir?"

"No. No, he died just like a man."

"Yes. Yes, I guess he did. Like a man. Not whining like this other lot." The centurion jerks his head towards the thieves. "That quake at the end was a lucky break for him, wasn't it?"

"Not for him. His reputation, perhaps. Doesn't do him any good at all, I'm afraid. Well. Wait until it's almost dark to take the bodies down." Decius scans the foot of the hill and points to the ditch. "I want his body dropped in at the north end and these two at the south. Guards at the south end. If his followers take the body after dark you didn't see anything. Got it?"

"Yes, Tribune." For an instant Decius thinks of adding a word or two of explanation but decides against it. He's already let discipline erode too far.

Later he reports to Pilate. They are in a small chamber behind the audience hall. Pilate is in an olivewood chair with a lictor on either side behind him.

"So. Decius," says the prefect. "Big fucking deal, wasn't it?"

"He didn't deserve to die."

"Right," Pilate sighs. "Right. He didn't deserve to die. Decius, how many men have you seen die? How many have you killed? Can you count them? No? No. Tell me now, how many of them deserved to die? All of them? No. None of them? Probably not. What difference did it make? You killed them because they were the enemy. You killed them because they were weaker than you. Only real capital crime so far as I know."

"You didn't say that to the Jews this morning."

"Yeah. Well. I thought hey, they're priests, maybe they take morality seriously." He laughs. "Funny. Nothing gives you latitude with right and wrong like thinking there's something out there making the rules. Like you can argue with him, or them, or it later on to square doing whatever it is you did. Knowing that this is all there is sharpens your perspective a little. Makes you remember that the only thing that lives after you is the memory of what you did and how well you did it." He shrugs. "And whether you did the right thing. But fuck it. Say. Did you let that crew of his make off with the body?"

Decius thinks about lying but won't. "Yes. I threw the body in the ditch but made it clear they'd have to wait until night to get it. I'm sorry, Prefect."

"Well. I'd call you an asshole except I'm a bigger one. I actually told them that they could put him in a tomb. And when the Talmud-thumpers came over to whine I told them to stuff it."

"Change of heart, Prefect?"

Pilate snorts. "Fuck, no. I gave the bastards what they wanted.

One dead carpenter. I wouldn't have given them that— bad mistake to let the subjects think they can push you around— but when they started shrieking about having no king but Caesar it was a no-choicer. I mean, if it got back to Tiberius that I didn't nail him up after that well, I'd be lucky to go the same way." He glances at his lictors. They leave. "Assuming, of course, that His Divinity can take his mind off the gallery of girls, boys, and in-between freaks he's got over there in Capri. Man knows how to retire."

He shakes his head. "Decius. Good work today. The job sucked. You did it like a soldier. I want you to do something more and I know you'll do that like a soldier too. I want you to take the guard for the next few days. Remind our stiff-necked monotheist friends that they scored one with their big man today and that they should just shut up and go figure out how to circumcise women or something. Wait." He laughs abruptly. "Don't, or they will. Just make sure they know their Governor respects their religion and expects them to respect his authority. Or I'll do to them what Yahweh did to Pharaoh."

Decius is startled. "Prefect? Prefect, you've been reading."

Pilate grins. "Hey. They don't make just anybody governor of the worst shithole in the Empire."

My vision used to encompass everything. Now it's shrunk down to a little circle of light in a sea of dark red. My ears roar with the sound of the blood coursing through my veins. Soon to stop.

In that little window into life I see my best friend, John. He was always closest to God. He was also closest to the edge. I can see from the way his eyes are rolling that this is going to put him over it completely. Too bad.

There is my mother. Why did she have to watch this, anyway? I would look at her but stubbornly my head refuses to move. All I see now is my toes, about a mile away. Better that way. Keep my head down. She'll think I'm unconscious. She would trade places with me in an instant.

Despite everything my head snaps up. She <u>would</u> trade places. That I knew. Not surprising. She was, after all, picked for this job. What surprises is the sudden realization that not just my mother, but any woman down there would trade places with her son up here. Any old geezer the same. Complaining, certainly. Hesitating not at all.

I look at the boys again. They are the same. Actually, more so. So few will come to a peaceful end. And they'll die not for their children or their wives but for me, and for an idea they will get completely wrong.

I look at John again. His eyes really are sticking out quite a lot. He's shaking. He won't look at me. He won't see things that are here, and soon he'll see so many things that aren't. Fantastic beasts with more crowns than heads to wear them; whores tattooed 666; the end of time; me with a list of grievances against the seven churches of Asia.

Breath comes quite hard now. There is a lot I can't feel. Parts of my body, I mean. This is not a mercy; all ordinary sensation is submerged and imperceptible under a rising tide of pain.

I keep thinking now it's crested, now it can't get any worse. Yet still it does. Someone has raised a sponge on a reed. My head turns without my willing it. Sour wine. I suckle it, hoping it will become what it's not through the simple exercise of my will. It's worked before, after all.

It doesn't this time. This is no wedding feast. Vinegar

remains vinegar. The clown with the sponge is laughing. Very funny. Why can't the boys ignore everything I've said about turning the other cheek and take care of him?

The anger rises and changes direction. Blame where blame is due. I roll my head upwards. The power of my voice is surprising. Mere audibility my last miracle. "Why me?"

The boys look startled. Then satisfied. This, after all, is part of their script, the part I couldn't quite rewrite for them. In this incomprehensible world all gods, their One as well as the others' Many, are capricious and cruel, spoken to only through the medium of spilled blood and the greasy smoke of sacrifice. The death of the innocent gives suppliant men some illusion of control. A ram buys a good harvest; a thousand doves averts a plague; a few hapless gladiators assure Rome's continuing Imperium.

And the best bargain of all, God's son dies and by this sacrifice saves all mankind.

Good deal. Great deal. Especially if you're not God's son.

Just minutes now. Clotted filth runs down the backs of my legs and recognizing it for what it is I burn with shame. I am prepared to die but I don't want my mother to see me fouling myself.

I start to cry. At this instant I am stripped even of my belief in who and what I am and have been, and I am left with only hope.

This is why I am here. This is why I have to die this way. Not as a sacrifice, but as a participant. Each one of them as they endure their trials will remember that God suffered as bad a death as their world had to offer. It buys them nothing but meaning. And that is enough. More than enough.

Or so I think. So I try to remember. I was God. Now I am just a man. And I am afraid.

The light was failing. An hour before Decius' men had pried the corpses off their lumber and thrown them in the ditch as he had instructed, the two thieves at one end and the rebellious teacher at the other. Still up on the hill, alone, Decius studied the north end through the growing dark.

Only moments after the body was pitched into the muck the dogs were on him. Within minutes the largest of the pack had claimed him as a prize. But once he had the body out of the ditch, onto firm ground where he could start working at the tender parts, the smaller dogs broke out of their circle and lunged in for a quick bite at the toes or fingers. So the big dog stood on the corpse's chest, teeth bared, daring his packmates to try for his meat.

The dead man's students stood in a cluster at the ditch's edge. Finally, one could stand it no more. He seemed to be their new leader. Decius recognized him as the man who had cost a soldier his ear the night before. He picked up a stone. Though it did the big dog no harm as it bounced off his head, it got his attention. Emboldened the leader threw another, and the dog crouched to face this new threat, his body splayed over his week's dinner.

The other students began an uneven stony rain. Their leader ran up the hill and in his barely literate Greek begged the use of the centurion's staff. Thus armed, he ran back down the hill and as the centurion laughed he swung the ivy rod into the dog like a war club, weeping with every stroke.

Though the dog was soon dead, the wooden staff did not

stop. Nor did the leader's sobbing. At last, the staff was thrown aside, and the other disciples' hands were empty. The leader hunched forward, crawling into himself, shuddering as he wept, his head resting on the ribs of the dead dog that lay over his teacher.

After a very long time he was still. The other students approached, cautious, but far bolder than the dogs who yelped and howled at the ditch's margin. The body was not too much the worse for wear. Decius watched as the students wrapped it in a shroud they had brought and bore it off.

"They forgot your staff, Centurion," said Decius.

His subordinate grunted. "Don't think I want it now, sir."

Decius smiled sourly. "I don't blame you."

"Extra wine for the men tonight, Tribune? They worked hard today."

They weren't the only ones, he thought. Pilate owed him now. Perhaps he would arrange for a transfer. Perhaps early retirement. He had, after all, been East for too long.

"You think so, Centurion?"

"Absolutely, sir."

Decius turned away. Sometimes he thought about Rome. Sometimes he wanted hot baths and the touch of silk against his skin. Sometimes he wanted to feel as though he was at the center of everything there was, of the only things there were. But today he thought that perhaps everything he saw was somehow less than everything there was.

A CALL TO ARMS

I couldn't be prouder of him if he was my own son.

He may be a little shorter, and a little heavier, than the other drummer boys. But he keeps his back straight as a ramrod and his face hard as stone, even when the twelve-pounders let rip and the Green disappears under white smoke from black powder.

A lot of colors there. The accidental poetry of war. As General Lee says, "It is as well that war is so terrible, or men would love it too much."

But I do not love it too much. Just enough. I stand at the head of my little company, the Fairfield Light Infantry, deployed in double-file, muskets at port-arms. A stiff breeze whips the smoke away, to reveal opposite, less than a hundred yards distant, fifty men in gray who mean to kill us, and whom we are meant to kill. A word of command, a sword raised by their officer, and their front rank drops to one knee. I lift my own sword and give the same order, with the same result. Between us, though, march the Union drummers, my own boy stumping gamely at their head.

I swallow hard. My duty is clear, regardless of my paternal feelings. I bark an order and fifty hammers click; fifty pieces level across a killing field through which a half dozen boys bravely keep their measured pace. My eyes swim, and I hope that if my boy is to fall, it will be quick.

A shout from the side opposite. "MEN OF VUH-*GIN*-YUH , H'OD YUH *FAH* UNTIL THOSE BRAVE BOYS ARE SAFE!" The Rebel officer waves his plumed hat in the air.

Grinning through my tears I lift my forage cap on sword point. "HUZZAH!" I cry. "THREE CHEERS FOR THE GENTLEMEN OF VIRGINIA!" My men respond with full-throated roar.

Within minutes the boys are safe behind our lines and ready to turn to their grim business of loading. A ragged volley of applause drifts to our ears from the edges of the Green, and I see the sun glint off phones as they video us. Whole families have come to watch the day's carnage safe in SUVs.

Just before the slaughter begins, I wave my boy up to me. I take off his forage cap and tousle his thick red curls, which I have never let him crop as his friends do. "You're in line for a promotion to the ranks, young feller," I say.

Stalwart, he says nothing. Yet the emotion betrays itself in the tautness of his jaw—still half-hidden in baby fat—and the swell of moisture in his blue eye. "Don't thank me now," I say, "and back to the rear and the powder with you—you're not a regular yet!"

With that I hear from the opposing ranks the cry of command and bark of a volley. My orderly flops forward, clutching at his throat as he has a hundred times before. The soccer moms and divorced dads at park's edge "Ooh" appreciatively. I raise my sword and bawl the order to fire.

The Battle of Westport has begun.

Okay, first, he's not my real dad.

Not that my real dad's not an asshole. Because he is. Not just because for the first twelve years of my life he never got home before I'd been asleep for three hours. But also because he fucked up my carefully planned shot at a pity handjob from the sitter by being caught boning her in the home theater. I didn't see dad a lot after that. Or the sitter. Which was too bad. She wanted me.

Mom's an asshole too. Not the same way as my real dad. She's an asshole who's there all the time. One day this kid Justin says hey, look, I got this cigar from my uncle. We pass it back and forth in the parking lot and we're both puking in five minutes. Justin got grounded for a week. Mom got me committed to Silver Hill. Inpatient. For three months.

When I got out I saw that she had plenty of time to rearrange her life. "Put 'er there, youngster, I'm yer noo dad." Jesus, what an asshole. For a couple of days, I pretty much stayed in my room until Mom told me that unless I got with the program it was back to the hospital and "something a little more aggressive." Which I guess meant four-point restraints and this new medication that could make you go blind and shit blood.

So I put the Xbox away and started to hang with Noo Dad.

I figured, how bad could it be? Most of my friends have new dads or new moms or two dads and two moms and they're all pretty much the same assholes.

Dude. How bad could it be? Check this out. Noo Dad had a hobby. Windsurfing? Nope. Marathons? Negative. Boning the au pair? 'Fraid not. No, my stepdad was a civil war reenactor.

Right. Like on the History Channel. The fat guys with red faces explaining flintlocks. And Noo Dad was a fat guy with a red face.

And a plan. He and Mom figured that I needed a little structured activity myself. And what could be better than joining Noo Dad's regiment as a drummer boy? Learn music, history, and close order drill at the same time?

I used to go to bed queasy on Friday night knowing he'd wake me up at dawn in his asshole costume with the feathers and sword and everything. And that he'd make me put on the same thing, but even dorkier, cheap-looking brass buttons hanging off dark blue wool stiff as cardboard and three sizes too big. All so that we could go to muster with his asshole friends and their kids who were the only losers in the world bigger losers than me. So we could bang our loser drums and load our loser stepdad's muskets.

After a couple of weekends like this it got so I didn't mind it too much. The marching sucked but the guns were cool and the stepdads didn't care if we fucked around with the gunpowder, blowing up anthills and water bottles, especially after they'd cracked the cooler along about ten with the first of many Civil War Bud Lights. They were pissed when Larry blew his eyebrows off, but as soon as he said he could see they said, oh okay, and went back to storming Vicksburg.

Usually Noo Dad took me to Starbucks on Main Street before we headed up into the Wilton Hills for our Saturday muster. He said we were bonding. I was usually trying to pretend that I wasn't sitting at a table with a fat guy with mutton chop whiskers, a sword, and a hat with red feathers coming out of it. And that I looked even worse.

It was usually okay, because nobody in Westport goes to the downtown Starbucks at seven o clock on a Saturday morning.

Except for this one day.

Lola Elliot is the hottest girl in the whole Middle School. She not only has tits, she has *big* tits. Justin says that she has a nipple ring. When I asked him how he knew, he told me that she let him play with it. But then he told me that it was because he was in the Post Office with his mother when Lola set off the metal detector. The security guard started laughing when he waved his wand over her boobs and Lola's mother got really mad when he kept waving it and laughing harder and harder and Lola started crying.

But Lola wasn't with her mom when she strolled into Starbucks this Saturday morning. No, she was with two other girls who would've been the hottest girls in middle school if it weren't for Lola. I couldn't figure out what they were doing at Starbucks during Designated Loser Time until I noticed the Saugatuck Rowing Club t-shirts and realized that they were on their way to meet their fellow Master Race Amazon Gods and Goddesses for a morning of healthy sweaty athletic fun.

Unlike me. Who was sweaty, okay, but only because I was wearing a heavy wool uniform in Indian Summer. And oh, I forgot, from shame.

I was trying to be as inconspicuous as you can be when you're sitting next to a man in a plumed hat sucking down a bucket of vanilla Frappuccino. Which isn't very. And which doesn't work, because the girls were nudging and giggling and because they were basically pretty nice girls trying hard not to stare but not succeeding.

Noo Dad reached the bottom of the tub and was wiping whipped cream from his moustache. "Friends of yours?" he asked.

"No. Yes. Kind of. Just girls at school," I said, staring at the table and praying that this wasn't the beginning of the avalanche.

"Sure are pretty," he said. "Why doncha' say hello? Show off the uniform. Women love a man in a uniform."

I kept staring at the table. A bead of sweat dropped from my forehead and spattered against the fake mahogany.

"I know," he said. "You're shy. I was young once too. Here, I'll help break the ice."

My eyes were screwed shut and my hands were over my ears. But I still heard the chair scrape across the floor and his boots shuffle as he stood up. Please God, I thought, let him just go over to chat and I'll run into the bathroom and Monday I'll tell one of their friends who's ugly enough to talk to me, oh, I was taking my demented uncle to an early Halloween party at Easter Seals and I got him some Starbucks to keep him quiet but he saw Lola and got all spastic.

But that didn't happen. Instead he grabbed my collar and pulled me to my feet. In the voice that he used to order volley fire, he said, "GOOD MORNING, LADIES."

The girls stopped talking. The baristas stopped talking. Coffee stopped brewing. Car ignitions died. Every bird in Fairfield County fell from the sky.

I dared to look up from my boots. The girls weren't laughing.

Noo Dad's right hand snaked over to his left hip. No, I thought. God, please, now, heart attack, brain tumor, meteor, whatever it takes. Let me die.

In the next second I became an atheist because God let me live to see it. Noo Dad launched his sword from its scabbard, raised the hilt to his nose, and swept it down in a salute that would've been the figure of grace anywhere but a coffee shop in

Westport on a Saturday morning. With his free hand he clapped me on the back. "Salute, boy," he growled from the corner of his mouth.

I'm an asshole. Or maybe not. He had a sword, after all. So I did as I was told.

The girls were backing towards the door. Lola was the last to make it through. Just before she left she returned the salute. And then she was in the municipal parking lot, doubled over laughing with her second- and third- biggest sets of tits in middle school friends. Right about then the manager was coming towards us saying, Umm, sir.

I guess this happened to him a lot because he got us out the side door and into the Blazer pretty fast. It was only ten miles to the muster but they were all windy roads so it took us half an hour. He kept talking the whole way about how tough it was to talk to girls but that was okay as long as you stayed true to yourself and your buddies. I was thinking about jumping out at a stoplight but I knew I couldn't run very fast in my uniform, and that anyway I'd be pretty conspicuous. As I was looking behind to see whether there was too much traffic to try it, I saw a brand new, black BMW 330 with this big guy who looked like he was maybe a junior behind the wheel. Sitting right next to him was Lola and her nipple ring. Her two friends were in the back.

I tried not to wet my pants. Not that it'd show through half an inch of Civil War wool. I got my iPhone out of my rucksack and cranked up Billie Eilish and slumped down in my seat as low as I could. After a while I guess Noo Dad got the message because his lips stopped moving and he slipped a fife and drum cassette into the dashboard. Cassette. It was a really old car. I kept one eye on the side mirror. The BMW stayed right behind us. I decided to try praying again.

Still didn't work. When we got to the Ridgefield Center Green there was a big sign for CIVIL WAR DAYS MUSTER. There were two little signs further up. Spectator parking to the left. Reenactor parking to the right. The BMW didn't go straight.

When we got to the reenactor camp Noo Dad told me he was going to give a little demonstration of Civil War firepower right after roll call. He wanted me to load all his pieces and take them to the center of the Green right in front of the bandstand. "Big day for you, boy," he said, tousling my hair so hard the iPod earbuds fell out. "You're going to be center of attention, front and center, handing the old guy his weapons." He leaned over and whispered in a voice they heard in Bridgeport. "Oh, and I see your friends from this morning came for the show." He pointed across the Green and I made myself look. There was Lola with the big guy and her friends.

I didn't want to hurt him. But I couldn't do this anymore. I loaded them all as fast as I could. And I can load fast. We did the drill every night after dinner and homework so I could have exactly one hour of TV or computer time. Hey, my pick.

I loaded them all the same way. Except his favorite. The light carbine, which I knew he'd use for the demonstration. That one I triple charged. Three paper cartridges. Three loads of gunpowder with three wads of paper and all the stones I could find rammed down the barrel as hard as I could. I ran them to the bandstand trailing arms and leaned them up against a rail. My hands were shaking when I got the percussion caps in place under the hammers and slid the safeties on. He was not going to get hurt, I kept saying. He was just going to get scared and stop doing this and leave me alone.

I knew I was disobeying orders leaving loaded weapons unattended. That meant a month without Xbox but I figured that wasn't going to be an issue in a couple of hours. So I ran over to where Lola and her friends were hanging out.

The big guy was really big. He might even have been a senior. He had chin pubes and a tattoo on his hand. I figured he was going to make this my perfect day by kicking my ass with Lola watching. But instead he just said, Dude, gave me a surfer cool nod, and walked off to where the other girls were getting chai.

So, it was just me and Lola. "I'm sorry my stepdad was such an asshole this morning," I said as fast as I could.

She played with her hair and said, "No, I'm sorry, I didn't mean to laugh. I wasn't laughing at you guys. I mean, I just never saluted before." Then she kind of giggled and didn't say anything else.

The silence went on. "Look, I know I look like a complete dork, but he makes me do this, and it's not my fault. He's not my real dad. Hey, my mom married an asshole and he makes me get dressed up like an asshole. So, I'm sorry about being an asshole with an asshole stepdad."

She was looking over my head. Which I guess wasn't hard because she was not only standing uphill but a lot taller than me. "Your stepdad isn't an asshole," she said. "*My* stepdad keeps walking into the bathroom when I'm in the shower. Once he had a camera."

I looked uphill. I couldn't see her eyes. But I did pop wood thinking about her taking a shower. I was going to ask about the nipple ring but decided now wasn't a good time.

After a minute she looked down at me. "So don't be too hard

on him. He's trying. Anyway, this is kind of interesting. I have to do a paper on the Civil War next week. You guys are cool."

"*What?*"

She played with her hair again. "Um, okay, cute. Hey, isn't that your stepdad at the bandstand?"

Noo Dad had the bullhorn in his hand. He was starting his lecture on nineteenth century small arms. The hand that didn't have the bullhorn had a carbine. That I'd loaded just right so that it'd go off like a grenade when he pulled the trigger.

"Uh—see you in school?" I said.

"Sure," she said. I'm pretty sure she smiled. Not certain because I was running back to the bandstand waving my arms in the air.

I have to say I was a little miffed with the boy for leaving live arms sloped at the bandstand, safeties or not. In the War Between the States that could've got a boy flogged at the least, hanged if there were plenty of recruits around to take his place. Even in today's "Don't ask-Don't tell" politically correct army he would've got a stern talking to.

But I turned all soft when I saw where he was running from. The cute little thing from Starbucks with the big hooters was waving as he bounced towards me.

And I forgave him completely when I heard what he was saying. "NO DAD NO."

He was out of breath when he pulled up beside me. I put my hand on his shoulder and raised the bullhorn. "AND NOW LADIES AND GENTLEMEN MY SON WILL DEMONSTRATE CARBINE FIRE."

He was shaking like a leaf. He almost dropped the piece when I put it in his hands. "Don't be nervous," I said, steadying it in his hands and placing the butt against his shoulder. "Your lady friend will be real impressed." I bent to his ear. "You never called me Dad before. Son."

The tears were running down his face and I guess they were running down mine too. As he lifted the carbine into firing position and cocked the hammer his thumb slipped and the percussion cap popped off the firing nipple. The hammer cracked down dry. "A LITTLE STAGE FRIGHT, LADIES AND GENTLEMEN," I said through the bullhorn. "WAR IS HELL."

The crowd laughed appreciatively. I thought I heard the boy saying words I'd tried to teach him not to say as I slipped a fresh cap under the hammer. I kept my hand on his shoulder as I said, "Aim high, son, just in case."

At the edge of the crowd I saw his ladyfriend waving. I took off my hat and waved back. "Now, son," I said, "fire!"

"Fuck," he said, and pulled the trigger.

It didn't hurt any worse than when Justin's brother Austin hit me in the head with a lacrosse stick. But Austin can really swing. And I guess maybe it was worse because lacrosse sticks don't burn all the hair off one side of your head and leave you permanently half deaf.

I don't remember the ambulance ride at all. In fact, I don't remember the first couple of days in the hospital except when I woke up to hear my mom saying it was time for Silver Hill again and Noo Dad saying he didn't care what the State Police said, it was an accident.

I guess they compromised because a couple of weeks later when I had my own room at Silver Hill, it was for post-traumatic stress disorder. I looked at my chart when the orderlies wheeled me down the hall for whirlpool therapy and left me alone for a long time. Mom was pushing for a lobotomy or at least electroshock every day until I could vote. Noo Dad said I just needed a little structure. The head shrink said that Noo Dad provided enough family support to justify release as soon as it was medically appropriate.

One day when I was down to just a couple of bandages around my head Noo Dad showed up. He wasn't wearing his Fairfield Light Infantry uniform. Instead he was wearing his Westport dad uniform. Much worse. Khaki dockers and a blue buttondown. Which isn't bad if you don't have muttonchop whiskers.

He was standing by the side of my bed with his hands behind his back. "Hey, son," he said.

"Hey. . .dad." I was worried that the stitches holding what was left of my ear on would let go.

"You rest up," he said. "I won't hold you up long. I just wanted to let you know something."

I was really afraid he was going to do the man love thing. All the guys at school come back gagging from weekends with real dads and stepdads.

He leaned over so close I could smell the Frappuccino. "Lola called," he said. "She wants to know how you're doing."

I figured I'd make a pup tent with the sheet but they had me on a lot of meds.

Because God hosed me again, Noo Dad didn't leave me in peace with the vision of Lola. Instead he said, "I can't give you the Purple Heart. Which I know you deserve, son. Taking that piece from my hands and taking the chance yourself. Knowing that the barrel was cracked but not wanting to embarrass us in front of all those people. And not wanting anything to happen to me. But even if I can't give you the Purple Heart, I can give you this."

He stood up and snapped to attention. His hands came from behind his back. He put an officer's hat with a scarlet plume on my head. It fell off against the pillow and after he tried to put it back a couple of times he just gave up and put it on the nightstand.

"Congratulations, Lieutenant," he said. He threw me a sharp salute, "See you on the battlefield soon."

He put his left toe against his right foot and did a perfect about-face. He left the room with his arms swinging.

I didn't say anything for a long time. There really wasn't any point. After a while I moved my head enough to look at the hat with the feathers. It really hurt.

"Thanks, Dad," I said.

I thought about it a little while longer.

"I am so fucked."

THE DARKNESS AT THE
CENTER OF EVERYTHING

Enmerkar had been watching the stick in the courtyard for a couple of days. He was pretty sure he was right about the shadow thing.

He was in the main court. Ahead of him was the gate, crowned with winged bulls with the heads of bearded men. Behind him loomed the ziggurat itself, a squat stepped pyramid whose flattened peak, ten yards above him, held the altar on which a sacrifice still smoldered.

The Sun God was just above the top of the temple gate. Hoping he looked as though he was polishing up a new prayer, Enmerkar held his hand up to the god and measured His distance from the arch. One hand's breadth. Good. He'd got it right. Earlier it was two hands.

He got to his feet. Bowing first to the Light of the World he went to the stick. His heart raced. He was on to something. What it was he wasn't sure, but it was definitely something. The stick's shadow had moved. He had marked it with a black stone when the god was two hands over the gate. Now at one hand he marked it with white. When it touched the gate he would mark it with red, just as he had done every day that week. But the pattern was clear.

Shalanum and Anunnaki looked worried. Enmerkar was either the gods' chosen messenger or a raging heretic. In the former case, disbelief meant an afterlife of forcible sodomy. By jackals. But if they believed him, and they were wrong, this life would end with impalement. After dismemberment. Tough call.

Shalanum was the first to speak. He was the senior, having become a priest just after Enmerkar himself, and ranked just below him. "Uh. . . . I'm not sure I understand that this has anything to do with the Destroyer of Night." All three prostrated themselves at the iteration of one of the Higher Names. When they rose, Shalanum was relieved to see that Enmerkar was still sufficiently orthodox to abase himself when propriety demanded. He was also a little amused to see that Anunnaki had overdone it again. The boy's nose was bleeding from the impact.

"You don't?" Enmerkar was irritated.

"Not . . . not quite." Shalanum knew that impalement hurt, and he didn't want to find out about the jackals.

"Well, look. The Sun God obviously makes these shadows follow him across the Vault of Heaven. Part of the way all nature worships Him." Enmerkar knew to put things that way, even though it made things take a lot longer to explain. He'd seen impalements too.

Anunnaki started to cry. "This. . . this is wonderful," he sobbed.

Enmerkar fought the urge to smack the novice. Another epiphany. He really didn't want to be around for the kid's first eclipse. "Yes," he said patiently. "It is wonderful. The Sun God's power defies belief. But here it is made manifest in a very subtle way. And even more wonderful, in a useful way."

"Useful?" Shalanum's voice took on an edge. He was the Temple Treasurer. A useful miracle could fill coffers.

"Useful," Enmerkar confirmed. "It looks as though there's a direct relationship between where the Sun God is in the sky and these shadows from the sticks. I don't know if the shadows will do the same things outside the temple courtyard— maybe the Sun God only does these things in His house, but I doubt it. I'll check . . ."

Enmerkar's mind had wandered, and he drew it back to the matter at hand. "I was thinking. Maybe we could use this so we could divide the day into parts that would be the same number, of equal length, wherever you were."

"Like a water clock?" Anunnaki was a twit, but he'd been to Uruk and seen what the artisans could do.

"Like a water clock. Only different. And better. Water clocks are all different. This would all be the same. The circle is always the same. It can always be divided into the same parts. And the Bringer of Life always follows the same course around it."

They were so carried away that they waited for him to finish his sentence before

they prostrated themselves and abraded their foreheads at the Highest Name. Even through a fresh layer of courtyard dust, Shalanum's raised eyebrows were visible. "This is wonderful. As the novice says. But how is it. . . useful?"

Enmerkar smiled. "Just think about it, friend. How do you think the peasants will see us once they know that we know exactly where the Burning One will be at every moment of every day? Impressed, don't you think?"

Shalanum smiled back. "Very impressed. I get it. I like it. Better than an eclipse."

"Not as dramatic. But more regular. It should really even out those peaks and valleys in the tribute flow."

Anunnaki looked confused. "I don't understand. How does that make it useful?"

Enmerkar and Shalanum exchanged a glance and sighed simultaneously. The boy didn't get it. But he was still a long way from his final consecration. Maybe once he was castrated he'd understand.

No one had heard Zarlagab approach.

"Enmerkar is overconfident," he said.

Damn, thought Enmerkar. *The old dungbeetle's been listening.* And obviously for a while. The High Priest was a constant irritant. Antiquity enhanced his authority all out of proportion to his intelligence. He had probably spat out his last tooth before Enmerkar was born. He was fifty at least.

Zarlagab stopped them halfway through the obligatory prostration. "Listen to what my grandfather told me his grandfather told him." Enmerkar kept a straight face. *Here we go.* "When my grandfather's grandfather was young the Highest and Brightest kept himself from us for three days."

"Behind clouds, Master?" asked Anunnaki. Enmerkar ground his teeth. *Of course not, you idiot.* Not even the High Priest was boring enough to tell a story about a rainy spell a hundred years ago.

"No, child," said the old priest gently. "I mean He did not rise."

Anunnaki began to cry. Again. Enmerkar wondered what was so bad about human sacrifice. The boy was aching for it.

Enmerkar's annoyance made him imprudent. "Master," he began, with what he hoped was deference, "if the Lord of Light hid Himself, how did your grandfather's grandfather know it was three days? Is not three days three risings and three settings?"

Zarlagab appeared unperturbed unless you knew him well. Enmerkar did. He suspected that the old priest was thinking about human sacrifice himself. And not of the novice. After a long silence in which Shalanum and Anunnaki looked anywhere but at Enmerkar the old priest replied. "He made three times. That is how he knew."

Enmerkar opened his mouth to question the reliability of the ancestral bowels, but thought better. "Oh. Of course. I see. Thank you, Master."

As the old priest droned on to the wide-eyed novice and obediently attentive treasurer, Enmerkar found himself wondering, as he often did, why it was that the world he experienced was as regular as the High Priest's great-great-grandfather. Why miracles and monsters were always so distant in time or space that he could never see them with his own eyes, or even talk to someone who had seen them himself. He was beginning to think that these tales from travelers and old men, and maybe even priests, were no more than fantasies to satisfy the weak-minded.

These were his most private thoughts. He planned to keep them that way. Impalement hurt.

Bismarck hit the snooze bar and rolled onto his back. Seven minutes. He usually set the alarm for half an hour before he actually had to get up so he could keep punching the button. He thought the sleep he got this way was his most pleasurable, if not most restful, because he got to fall asleep four or five times just before getting up.

Not this morning. When the alarm went off the second time he noticed two things out of the ordinary. First, what was usually Imus was today mere static. The second thing was even odder. It was dark. Completely dark at seven in the morning. In March. Well, hell, he'd obviously mis-set the alarm the night before. Good. This meant another couple of hours of sleep.

Careful to keep the comforter between himself and the cold bedroom he scrunched towards the night table like a two-hundred-pound inchworm. It was hard to see the glowing digital numbers with his glasses off.

What the fuck? Seven-oh-nine.

He'd been married long enough to know who to blame. "Goddammit, Carol, what did you do to the clock?"

She replied from somewhere under a foot of down. "Nothing. And goddammit yourself, what time is it?"

"How the hell should I know?"

"By looking at the clock two inches from your face, Einstein."

"Well it won't do any good because someone's been screwing around with it. It says seven-ten."

"It can't be seven-ten. It's pitch black."

"Thank you Carl Sagan. Shit. Now the goddamn dog's awake."

The dog was bouncing around as energetically as anything with a full bladder could. Bismarck knew that resistance was pointless. He put on his glasses, rolled out of bed, and pulled on some sweats. Bitching faintly under his breath he shuffled into the kitchen for the leash.

What the hell was this, a digital conspiracy? Both the coffeemaker and stove clocks said seven-twelve. But he could still see stars from the window over the sink. Maybe a power surge. But why would that make the clocks run fast?

He took the dog into the back yard. Well, regardless of the real time, the dog sure was acting like it was the end of a long night. Come to think of it his own lower quadrant was kind of full.

As the dog snuffled and squatted Bismarck studied the night sky. There it was, the new comet, the one that had entered the Solar System just two months before and now was the second-brightest thing in the night sky. It was right over the chimney, exactly where it had been when he'd walked the dog just before bed.

That didn't seem right, somehow. Why he wasn't sure. Well, there was the same half-moon, right at the horizon, exactly where it had been before bed.

Wait a second. He looked at the comet again. Exactly where it had been at midnight. And the moon. Just the same. Had he been asleep fifteen minutes? But the dog was dumping away as though he'd had a full night to digest. And dammit, it felt like morning. He ran his hand across his face. It rasped.

He looked back at the comet. Then back to the moon. His hands began to shake.

Enmerkar stared at his stick. There was a problem here. The Sun God had abandoned the sky to His pale spouse some time before. And she was in one of her monthly moods. As wives will have, Enmerkar realized, or thought he realized, making due allowance for the physical alterations that had fitted him for the highest orders of priesthood. So, She wasn't shining either.

Which meant the stick cast no shadow. Which meant that in the time-dividing business it was pretty much limited to half the day. And only sunny days. Which in Chaldea, fortunately, were plentiful.

Distracted, he didn't hear Zarlagab come up behind him. "You didn't believe me," said the old priest.

That was usually true about just about anything, so Enmerkar temporized. "Of course I believed you, Master. About what?"

The old priest smiled sourly. "You come so close, Enmerkar. You'll go so far if you come no closer. Watch that tongue. I can have it cut out without checking with Uruk."

Enmerkar kept his face a smiling mask. Legally Zarlagab was right. Politically he was wrong. Enmerkar had lots of friends in Uruk. All of whom liked to hear him talk. Which he couldn't do without a tongue.

"Master, what did you think I didn't believe?"

The old man smiled again. "Don't be coy, child. The three days' darkness."

"Ah . . . That. Well . . ."

"I didn't tell you enough. I didn't tell you why it happened."

No doubt because it didn't happen, Enmerkar thought. He kept silent and tried to look reverent.

The old man, satisfied, continued. "There was a long-haired star in the Vault of Heaven. I know our best men don't agree on what they are. They always mean disaster, though, on that all concur."

Enmerkar kept his smile within. When still a very young priest he realized that every disaster that accompanied heavenly disturbance was entirely man-made, and always the result of simple panic.

Zarlagab went on. "I subscribe to the Hittite belief that comets are the Highest One's concubines. When they get too close he must hide Himself in order to avoid the anger of his wife."

Ashur had heard that one too. He thought that it was scarcely surprising that the Sun God kept concubines if he and the Moon Goddess were never in the same place at the same time. Sometimes when he lay awake when the other priests snored around him he wondered in thoughts he was afraid to hear whether the sky was peopled at all, whether the gods and goddesses to whom he devoted his life and sacrificed his manhood even existed. Then he became more afraid still. Alone he thought that perhaps the Sun God was a hot stone and the Moon Goddess a cooler one, and his studies of the turning sky made him wonder whether each of its lights was a smaller, dimmer hot point fixed to some kind of celestial wheel.

But comets frightened him, because they came from nowhere and returned to nowhere without order or predictability. Then real fear as he realized that his thoughts would be read to him after he died and he would suffer for each.

But as the old priest droned on, something occurred to him. He and the other priests knew the courses of the stars, each traveling different but knowable routes. Perhaps these comets were different only in that their courses were longer. Maybe if he looked at temple records he could see a pattern. Maybe talking to old people would shed some light.

He smiled at the chief priest. He would ask questions. The old man would be pleased.

Bismarck could see that Carol was about ten seconds from calling 911.

"Look," he said. He sounded pretty calm in his own ears and he hoped in hers too. "I know it sounds nuts. But look at the clock. What does it say?"

She made a big production of looking. "Seven-forty-five."

"Right. And it's still dark. What does that lead you to conclude?"

"Something wrong with the clock?"

"Could be. Now look at this." He showed her his watch. "What does this say?"

"Seven forty-six. Something wrong with that too."

"Right. Now give me your hand." He carefully drew it across his face. "What do you feel?"

"Your face."

"Right. What's on it?"

"Beard."

"Lots of beard?"

"Usual amount for morning."

"Exactly. Exactly." He wagged his head in satisfaction. "The usual amount for morning. Yet it's still dark. Hmm."

She was starting to look seriously scared. Either it was beginning to sink in or she was wondering whether she was going to wind up in lots of separate ziplocks in the freezer.

"When I was walking the dog," said Bismarck, "did you go back to sleep?"

"No."

"Aha." Despite the terror he was struggling to suppress, he was enjoying this. His mind was still working just fine. "What did you do?"

"I went to the bathroom."

"And?"

"Well, Jesus, honey, I peed."

"Good. Very good. A lot?"

"A normal amount."

"A normal amount for what time of day?" He knew that she was beginning to understand. She normally couldn't stand it when he cross-examined at home.

"A normal amount for the morning. No this is ridiculous. Let me see if I can find something on the radio so we know what time it is for Christ's sake. And then we really need to talk." She fumbled at the side of the bed. Bismarck felt fear for the first time since he'd come back into the house. If it really was still nighttime he was in big trouble. She'd been getting more and more strident lately about too much time at the office and too much wine at dinner.

Imus was still off the air. She switched to an FM preset. NPR.

Noah Adams' voice momentarily drove the chill deeper into his gut. If he was right how could these guys be working? Then he relaxed. If Morning Edition was on it was, well, morning. It didn't occur to him just then that there was something basically wrong with his perspective if the suspension of natural law and near certain global catastrophe were cause for relief.

Noah sounded only marginally less calm than usual. He was talking to someone. Well of course, it was radio; what else would he do?

"—Ira, is it possible that this is temporary?"

Ira Flatow, the science correspondent, didn't sound nearly as collected. "How the hell should I know?"

Noah was a pro, no question about it. He just rolled on. "Is it possible that this has something to do with the comet that first became visible just last week?" he asked. "For example, could it be exerting enough of a gravitational pull to stop the Earth?"

You could almost hear Flatow roll his eyes. "Not even remotely. I mean, forget that a comet's just a big goddamn snowball without enough gravity to keep a gerbil from jumping off it. Forget that if it did have enough gravity to stop a goddamn planet tidal forces would have pulled the earth into a zillion asteroids over the course of months or years not to mention distorting the orbit of every other planet when it was still half a light year away. Just think simple physics. The earth weighs fourteen septillion tons. At the equator it rotates at a thousand miles an hour. Imagining for just a second that you stopped something that big and that fast, all that kinetic energy would turn into heat. Boom. They'd see the flash in the Andromeda Galaxy three million years from now."

Noah was holding it together pretty well. "Uh, you mentioned the other planets. Are they still . . . behaving normally?"

Ira laughed a little. "Normally? Yeah sure I guess. I mean if you mean by 'normal' they're still obeying natural law and turning on their axes, well, yes, I'd have to say they were."

Ira kept laughing. Bismarck's stomach began to knot a little. It knotted more when the sound from the radio stopped sounding like laughter and instead began to sound like something else. Bismarck hadn't heard it very often, at least not like that; it was the kind of thing you hear at funerals of old women coming from husbands of fifty years, tough old guys who'd come of age on beaches at Iwo and Anzio and Normandy who now suddenly found themselves alone with the darkness at the center of everything. Face to face with a universe without meaning or mercy.

Maybe Noah didn't really have it together. He was letting it happen instead of cutting to a pledge drive. Coffee mugs and totes for the end of the world.

Slowly Ira recovered himself in sniffles and hiccups. Noah was gentle. "What can we expect?"

"How the hell should *I* know? How should anyone? You don't understand. This just can't be happening. It means that everything we thought we knew was wrong. Everything we've known for three thousand years. All wrong." He was getting close to the edge again. "Maybe if we just believe. Maybe this is the Universe testing our belief. Maybe if we believe in science really really hard this will stop."

Bismarck had been thinking. He was starting to wonder what the next couple of weeks were going to be like. It still looked like midnight outside. That meant that it was noon on the other side of the world. And that it had been for quite a while. That hemisphere was going to start getting pretty hot after forty-eight hours or so of uninterrupted midday. Which meant that sooner or later he was going to start getting pretty cold. But then that hot air would begin to flow around from the daylight side of the world and collide with the frigid air over Hartford and the weather would probably start getting really weird.

But that all assumed that the world was still working the same way. Except for this one glaring exception.

Ira was right. Everything we thought we knew was wrong. Bismarck's hands resumed their tremor. What if he went out into the yard right now and saw the trees uprooting themselves and walking towards the river? What if he heard the flowers talking to one another? What if Carol walked to the kitchen on hooves and brought him coffee with talon hands?

Carol. Carol was curled into a fetal ball. "Please believe. Honey, please believe. Please. This can't happen. This is a dream. Please make it stop. We have to believe. Do like the man said. If we believe it has to stop."

Enmerkar looked up from his stick. The old priest was watching again. Enmerkar had made him happy with his questions. He decided to continue on the same tack. "Please, Master, how did your great-great-grandfather act when the Brightest One hid himself?"

Zarlagab smiled. "How would anyone? He was terrified. He thought that it was the end of everything. As one day it will be. But not then."

"But what did he do? What did his people do? Did they sacrifice?"

The old man shook his head. "No. People at the end of their lives and their children's lives and their grandchildren's can't think. They can only believe. So they huddled together and believed. And the Sun God came back."

Enmerkar turned his head in time to hide the smile. What a surprise.

Sunlight was streaming through the window when Bismarck awoke. Bright and hot. Foggily he thought to call the office with a story about a flu. Or a power failure that killed the alarm clock.

The clock. It all came rushing back. Oh my God. It was over. The earth had moved. How long, he wondered, had he and Carol lain there quivering, faces buried in each other's necks, begging the world to go back to the way it was supposed to be like five-year-olds praying for a broken vase to unbreak, for the past to unhappen.

He looked to his left. Carol was still stuporous, her face lax and tearstained. Disentangling himself as gently as he could, he moved to the radio. First rolling the volume down to the lower threshold of audibility he turned it on.

Noah again. Tired but not nearly as edgy. "Ira, just how could this virus have affected every digital clock in the world?"

Ira laughed. A real laugh, effervescent with relief. "Noah, once the hacker cops have tracked this one down computer science will take a fifty-year Great Leap Forward. This makes the Michelangelo bug look like something from Radio Shack. It must have been dormant in every chip made for the past ten years at least. Self-replicating. And absolutely universal. No digital clock in the world told the right time yesterday."

Noah sounded just skeptical enough. Always a pro. "Wait a second, Ira. My wristwatch isn't digital. And it told the same time as all the digital clocks. And I felt just as hungry when I woke up as though I'd slept through eight hours."

Ira laughed again. His pleasure was radiant, like a saint's ecstasy at a vision of heaven. Bismarck imagined him crowned with a halo and levitating four feet off the studio floor in the full lotus position. "That's the real genius of this whole thing. Of course you did. The Unahacker who set this up knew that the whole world runs to digital time. How many digital clocks do you have in your house? Half a dozen? Coffeepot, radio, microwave? And when you saw them all telling the same time you just imagined your analog watch was telling you the same thing. And your stomach too. Just like you ignored the fact that it was still dark and assumed your computer clocks were right."

Noah knew the script. "All right. But what about those reports from observatories that the stars weren't moving?"

"Appearing to move," Ira corrected. God he was full of piss and vinegar. "That's the scary thing. Even people who should have known— who did know— that the Earth couldn't just stop panicked and started to reconcile all the evidence the wrong way. Panic is a terrible thing." He paused. "I mean, you heard me."

"Less said the better," said Noah. "So Ira, how did the Unahacker pull this off?"

'Well, Noah, we don't know. In fact there's no evidence at all as to how he did it. But we know he had to do it, that *someone* had to do it. Because if it didn't happen that way then the Earth did stand still. And as I explained last night that can't happen."

Bismarck rolled onto his back. For a moment he almost laughed himself, relishing the Unahacker's brilliant conception and superhuman execution. Then he remembered Carol shuddering and sobbing. How close he had felt to madness. He hoped they caught the bastard. He hoped they didn't bother with a trial.

Carol snored softly. He thought to wake her with the good news. But let her rest a little more.

Something small and cold stirred in the pit of his stomach. What if there wasn't a Unahacker after all? What if the Earth had just stopped and started for no reason? What if it happened again?

With an effort he slowed his panicked breathing. Crazy talk. It couldn't happen. Anxiety attack. He was sure everyone would have them for weeks and months to come.

In a minute he would call the office. Just now he would lie there and feel the earth turn.

The temple's walls were a quarter of a mile away. Enmerkar settled as comfortably as he could. He had a while to wait. He didn't mind. He would be able to hear the gongs and trumpets of midmorning prayer from where he sat. If the stick cast its shadow at the same point he'd marked on the tablet at midmorning prayer the day before, in the temple, he'd know he was right. He knew he was on to something.

CROSSED WIRES

Frobisher thought he was too young to have a mistress. Also, too cool. Mistresses were for old guys with pinkie rings, fat tanned guys jammed into Speedos. He saw them at beaches everywhere, East Hampton to St. Bart's. They hunkered in folding chairs shrieking through cellphones to garment district offices while bits of lemon chiffon in thongs worked sunblock into their hairy shoulders or sprawled before them topless, like deer tied to hunters' bumpers.

But that wasn't Frobisher. Frobisher had been born the day Bobby Kennedy was assassinated. He couldn't remember a world before color television. He was an architect. His partners were women. He wore clothes from Paul Smith. He got into Pilates while most of his friends were still doing blow. In short, not the kind of guy to have a mistress.

He expended a lot of intellectual energy trying to find other things to call Amber. Most of them were pretty much excluded by the hard fact of his marriage. Married guys couldn't call anyone a "significant other." And girlfriend would have been out even if he hadn't been married. So usually he just settled for "friend." It was literally correct, or so he thought most of the time, except for those not-infrequent occasions when his viscera churned over her chance use of an MTV adjective to describe a CNN event. It was inclusive rather than exclusive. And sometimes it gave him the advantage of pretending to a sexual orientation other than his own, not a bad thing in his line of work, in which a man's "friend" often had a pierced scrotum.

That morning he was in his office writing Amber a little love email. It was a Saturday, so he felt comfortable taking a few minutes away from the proposal he was drafting. He also felt comfortable with the gold hoop in his ear and the Ted Baker shirt and the Strokes on the iPod. He pulled up the browser his firm had carefully and expensively customized, pulled down a menu, and clicked Compose.

Darling—

I want to tell you exactly what I want to do next time I see you. I'm not going to say a word. I want you to come to the door with nothing on.

I'm going to push you to the couch and make you sit. Then I'm going to kneel in front of you and spread your legs and hook them over my shoulders.

Then I'm going to lick you exactly the way you love to be licked. Do you remember that weekend —

A knock on the door. Shit. His partner Stephanie was hovering outside the glass wall mouthing "have to talk to you *now*." Oh well. He tried to look businesslike and held up a finger. One minute. Finger still up he swung the mouse around and pulled down the personal address book. Stephanie knocked again, hard this time. Just as he clicked send.

Stephanie as usual had turned a minor administrative glitch

into a seminar on firm culture. With particular emphasis on how everyone was feeling. While Frobisher actually kind of liked these little seances—it was as close as he'd ever come to menstruation—he found himself unaccountably impatient this once. Unaccountably, until he realized that Steph was cutting into his Saturday afternoon gym time, which always segued into a workout with Amber.

After his third glance at the Tag Heuer, Steph finally got the message. Leaving him free to pack the Mac into the messenger bag and head to the Apogee.

Frobisher had loved the Apogee at first sight. It looked like the kind of gym where Frank Gehry could chat up a Diesel Jeans model. Everything was brushed chrome and oiled wood and matte finishes. Absurdly mesomorphic figures who might just have stepped off the Elgin marbles strained discreetly at futuristic machines whose purpose could only be surmised, even when in use. Foreign men with towels and squeegees and sprays kept the place from smelling like what it was, unheeded by furiously pedaling stockbrokers.

And hey, what about the babes. Frobisher still had days when he thought every woman in New York was beautiful. When his friend Drake introduced him to the Apogee three years before, two years into his marriage, frustrated lust and consequential depression had been making him stop to stare disconsolately at Victoria's Secret posters in the subway. Walking into the Apogee was like the first really gorgeous spring day on Union Square except that all the beautiful women were in Spandex jogbras. Frobisher joined at once.

There was, of course, a down side. He had never been that much of an athlete. More like a twice a week jogger who upped it to every other day when his inseam bit into his prostate when he crossed his legs. But he usually felt pretty good about the way he looked. Here, though, it was a very bad day indeed if he was the third best looking heterosexual male over thirty. On the other hand, it was an equally bad day if the tenth best looking woman there didn't look like a fourteen-year-old's wet dream.

He had first met Amber there. Or had first seen her, at least. Drake pointed her out. Not an introduction, really, but it obviously made Drake feel avuncular ever after. Amber was working out on the Butt Blaster. Before that moment Frobisher would have thought a Butt Blaster was a guy who'd spent a lot of time in prison. But no, it was an exercise machine. Amber was working muscles Westport wives didn't know they had and didn't want to know about anyway. She was wearing black spandex.

Drake looked impressed. "Jesus," he said. "Look at that. I'll bet she could snap the neck off a Coke bottle with that thing."

She had chosen that instant to look up. She struck Frobisher the way a truffle strikes a starved hog. Indeterminate ethnicity—vaguely Asian, possibly Puerto Rican, certainly not Wonder Bread. Heart-shaped face, lots of thick black hair, skin the color of his habitual skinny latte's, white white teeth with an immediately endearing gap. And Drake was right about the back yard.

Drake had gone off to find an audience for his biceps routine. Frobisher smiled at her. She smiled back. At a loss as to what to do next, Frobisher stood there a full five seconds before running like a rabbit. When he realized that he was hoping that she hadn't noticed his wedding ring the guilt felt like a lump of cold grease in his duodenum.

He couldn't get her out of his mind that day or the next. He'd had these little crushes before. They were part of his experience of marriage. At least marriage to Kristin. Which he often thought of as life in the J. Crew catalogue. Kristin was beautiful in exactly that way. Not like one of the light-skinned women of color in the swimsuit section the producers threw in to lend a gloss of forbidden sensuality; no, she was like one of the Gwyneth Paltrow-types in the front, with the hundred-dollar sweaters, beaming at a much older barn-jacketed hubby while baby and Labrador pup rollicked at her feet.

She was also pretty much sexless. Not averse to it. She just didn't like it all that much. It was something that happened because it had to, periodically, like some of the cruder bodily functions, possibly yielding satisfaction but never real pleasure. She had always been that way. Frobisher had thought that maybe when they were married, she would become so secure in their relationship that her sexuality would blossom. Instead it got neither better nor worse. For a while he tried to get her to his way of thinking. Once he left the shower to find her in the hallway wearing nothing but a t-shirt. She was standing in front of a full-length mirror. Thinking that fortune favors the brave, he had slipped his hands under the shirt and over her breasts and begun to nuzzle her neck. Immediately erect, he had gently, or so he thought, pushed her forward so that he could enter her standing from behind while they faced the mirror. At the moment of orgasm, he had looked at her face in the mirror. Instead of eyes locked on his in mutual passion he saw a face screwed shut. In the moment afterwards he felt like a rapist. She told him she had felt degraded.

For weeks afterwards he was too confused and ashamed to

touch her. Ashamed, because he thought he had acted like a caricature male; confused because he was, after all, male. It was then that the conviction began to grow that there was something wrong at the core, either with him or the marriage. He started to act as though it was he. First came the covert visits to websites with names like spoogetarget.net or hotblaxxx.com. Only at home; he knew enough about networks to dread the possibility that one Sunday morning Stephanie would log in from her Rhinebeck barn to find her partner linked to teentitties.org.

So instead, on a few Friday evenings, well after Kristin's ten o'clock bedtime—doctors rise early—he hunched over his monitor with a wad of Kleenex in one hand and his mouse in the other. A date he would have turned into a long-term relationship had it not been for Kristin's periodic scans of the History menu. Which he countered with a fable, fortuitously torn from that Thursday's "Circuits" section of the Times, about former Soviet hackers who were seizing Western PCs on the behalf of Moscow pornographers. Which Kristin at first gave all the credit it deserved, but gradually came to accept over the months in which he told their friends, over coffee or pizza, about the Chechen porno crime lords who had temporarily surfaced in southern Fairfield County.

Having dodged the bullet, he knew the internet was out. Unless he wanted to buy shrink wrapped copies of "Juggs— Home of the DDD" from Pakistani 7-11s along Route 1, park next to the Dumpster, and squeal off to the Merritt once he'd found paradise under the dashboard lights, he'd have to think of another venue.

Thus, he was in the video store of a Friday night. As he pretended to study the box of a subtitled romance his eyes were drawn to the back room. He had never passed through that discreet doorway, thinking that he might as well walk around with a Loser sign on his back. But tonight, he edged towards it like a shoplifter, eyes scanning French farces and lost classics, lips silently moving as he rehearsed his cover story. "What? Isn't this where they keep the Jarmusch? Look, have you ever heard of an Iranian director called Kirostami? Like Kirosawa and they sound alike ha ha ha."

But it was unnecessary. Inside there was no one else. His heart sank. Worse than discovery was the prospect that everyone else in Westport was out getting laid at that very moment. Well, move quick. Jaw muscles clenched with shame he showed up at the checkout with "Romancing the Bone" tucked between "Life is Beautiful" and "To Have and Have Not." He could always claim the clerk had made a terrible mistake. But he got home without incident. After making sure Kristin was asleep, he crept into the study, popped the disk into the DVD, and took a wrong turn off Cool Street before the Coming Attractions were finished.

Eventually he was desperate enough to confide in Drake. Big as Frobisher was on sharing and caring, the prohibition against discussion of sexual failures was hardwired into the male brain long before bipedal locomotion was more than a sometime thing.

It was particularly difficult with Drake. Drake was the last of the old-time cads. An Edwardian rake, rapier-thin in the scabbard of a Zegna suit; a triathlete despite a cigar habit that predated Gordon Gecko. But he was also fifty. Confession to someone half a generation his senior was somehow less painful.

Drake had not been helpful. At least, in the short run. "So the problem is you're not getting enough."

"I don't like to put it that way. I just want to have a complete relationship."

"You also want to get laid more. Or am I missing something?"

"You're not missing something," Frobisher conceded bitterly. "I don't know what to do. Do you know any therapist I could call?"

Drake rolled his eyes and guillotined a Macanudo. "For you? Since when does wanting to get laid rate a shrink?"

Frobisher blinked hard. "For us."

Drake sighed. "Kid, I hate to break this to you. In fact, I resent having to break this to you. Your father should have told you. I hate having to act like anyone's father unless I'm so adjudicated. But anyway. Here's the hard fact. People are who they are. Particularly that way. There is this thing called the bell curve. Some people are on the right-hand side. They want it all the time in all the ways they can figure out that won't put them in the hospital, at least for very long. In that category, I am happy to include myself. On the left-hand side are people who basically don't care one way or the other. They're equally happy. Or can be. And for every person on my side there's someone on the left side. And of course, there are all the variations in between. But by and large, most of the time you are where you are. Like with IQ, or height. A constant. Of course, it's more complicated than height, but the individual baseline tends to stay pretty much the same."

Frobisher looked stricken. "So it's not going to get better."

Drake drew on the cigar. "Sorry, kid. You are where you are."

"And it's not my fault?"

"Nope."

"So what can I do?"

"Well, basically, not much. Except make some decisions. About who you are and what you want." He studied the ash at the end of his cigar as though he'd never seen such a thing before. "Kristin is a lovely woman and I like her very much." Kristin, of course, hated Drake. "But life zips by pretty fast and I'm advised it's one to a customer."

It was a week later that Frobisher saw Amber.

Before Kristin started thinking about marriage, she sneered at friends and acquaintances, and sometimes even total strangers fortunate enough to have their nuptials published in the Times, who dumped half their identities and changed their names just to join the world of the Cleavers. But as she approached the actual moment of engagement—no proposal, naturally; mutual decision long discussed—she found herself idly doodling out a new name for herself. And damn if it didn't sound pretty good: Kristin Frobisher. It had the imposing yet feminine ring she always associated with Eurotrash. She could see herself in a foreign-language Vogue.

That was the great thing about Frobisher. He always made her think of exotic magazines. Huge ten-dollar glossies in French or Italian about design or furniture or photography. When she was in medical school surrounded by former science majors in Dockers, he would meet her post-call looking like something out of the British GQ. She liked that. She had been a science major and no matter how good she looked she felt grubby and dull in medical school. It probably had something to do with not sleeping very much and not being encouraged to think very much either. She always hoped that she wasn't anything like every person she spent every waking moment with.

Frobisher made her think she wasn't. He had a cool old car and friends with interesting haircuts. They talked about something other than medicine and money. The medicine part didn't surprise her; the money part did. One weekend a month she was let out of her cage and Frobisher took her to museums and bars in the City and they would go back to his apartment and make love until it was time for her to go back to New Haven.

When they got married, she thought it was still new. It was, but only because they didn't know each other. Her friends told her not to worry. No one knows the other in that first year, or in the first five. Kristin was reassured. But not for long. She added up the monthly weekends and weekly overnights and realized that in two years of dating she'd spent about two months with this guy she was suddenly introducing to realtors as her husband. And she wasn't exactly sure how crazy she was about that. She also wasn't too sure about being married to a guy who earned just enough to cover his wardrobe, even if it was really cool.

So that Saturday she spent the morning at the hospital and came home to what she thought of as most expensive three-bedroom cape Earth. Her fillings hurt every time she looked at it. Frobisher had sold her on it with painful earnestness. It was not just an aesthetic statement; it was an investment in his career and their future. But why it was necessary to buy an already hideously overpriced Fairfield County hutch, gut it at great expense, and then build out to the property line was beyond her. Especially when the end result looked like a collaboration between Sir Christopher Wren and George Jetson.

She settled into an ergonomic chair designed for robots and dug in for an afternoon of surfing. She didn't know exactly why she spent so much time on the Web. Maybe radiologists just like looking at screens. Ten years before she'd probably have been at a video arcade.

Mail first. Hey. Something from the husband. Big news no doubt. Honorable Mention in the Unbuildable Chickencoop Competition. She swung the mouse and clicked Open.

Five minutes later her cheeks were still burning.

Frobisher was never able to pinpoint when every Saturday went from elation to despair. But it always happened. He was pretty sure he emitted a glow you could read by the time he got on the train at Grand Central. At the 125th Street stop he always had a smug satisfied smirk. But by Stamford he always twitched with anxiety.

This Saturday he was radiant as he dropped into his seat and popped open his bottle of Glaceau. That gave him a secret dirty pleasure that he always saved for his weekend ride home. The bottle had a recessed nipple mounted on its bulbous mammary top. It could be pulled out with the teeth and suckled. Just like Amber. The caps were color-coded to clue you in to the calorie-free fruit essences flavoring a substance otherwise indistinguishable from drippings from a defrosting Frigidaire. Even though he didn't really care for Mountain Black Cherry, he always bought it just to add a little visual verisimilitude to the memory he savored for the next forty-five minutes.

Actually, less than forty-five minutes. By the time the train crossed into Connecticut the familiar little worries had begun. The real fear began as the train slowed for his station. Jesus, what if Kristin saw the claw marks on his back? Or tooth marks on his thigh? On the first nights he was careful to sleep in sweats, never thinking that they were harder to explain in August than semen-stained boxers in the laundry hamper. On those nights he lay rigid, dreading the possibility that on this one goddamn occasion she'd decide she wanted to screw.

He needn't have worried. She never did. By late Sunday afternoon, the usual occasion of their conjugal visit, abrasions and conscience were sufficiently healed for him to perform unhindered. During the week, his anxieties were a little less direct. And a lot more global. Like what the hell was he doing, anyway? He had this great life partner he really respected and who supported and understood his work and every Saturday afternoon he was rolling around with someone who had a Lil' Kim poster taped to the refrigerator and teddy bears on her bed.

Once when a rail strike had stranded him in the City, he had spent a whole night with Amber. Exhausted, he had watched her pad naked around the bedroom like a multiracial succubus from a harem dream. She flipped on the TV, picked her channel from the tabloid atop it, and snuggled up beside him and held him tight. "America's Funniest Pet Home Videos" sort of broke the spell. He had found work out of town the next few weekends.

But come back he did. There was no mystery to it. He and Kristin always finished in the same position they started in. He and Amber didn't finish in the same room. Sometimes he wondered where she'd learned this stuff. Not in a book, that was certain. Maybe a video. Maybe it was just a talent. He didn't really need to know.

Westport. Frobisher didn't like living there all that much. It was too suburban. Sometimes when he and Kristin drove to the City on weekends, he felt that his Connecticut plates were stuck to his back like a Kick Me sign. He knew that somehow the bartender at Void guessed that he went home not to a SoHo loft but something with topsoil and property taxes and the sleepy fog that blew in over bridges. He was afraid that one day he would find an Access or a Zagat on his coffee table and that would be it for his self-esteem.

But at least he had the house. As always, his heart beat a little faster and he sat a little straighter as he rounded the corner on the drive back from the station. It stood out from its neighbors like a pedigree at the pound. Ironic and postmodern, it had inspired one reviewer to describe it as a Real-Life bungalow. Frobisher tried never to remember that another had described it as architecture with a sound bite attention span.

The switchbacked front walk meant that visitors had a lot of time to enjoy the fusion of Zen rock garden and English herbary that took up his pocket-sized front yard. It also meant that he had a lot of time to wonder why the front door was visibly ajar. This was not like Kristin. Maybe she'd just arrived. Or maybe he'd just been burgled, but the alarm would've blown all the leaves off the trees.

He pushed the door aside a little diffidently. If he had been burgled, he wasn't really excited about facing a trashed living area. Or if not, Kristin. He hated facing her fresh from an hour and a half with another woman. He was always sure that he would give himself away. His voice a little too cheerful, his inquiries just a little more solicitous than circumstances warranted.

Well, burglars probably wouldn't have thrown on a Billie Holliday CD for background music. And there she was. Her back to him, swaying a little to the music. Oddly enough, wearing the silk robe he'd bought her two Christmases before and had never seen since. Must've just showered or something.

He dropped his gym bag on the floor and revved up for his husband-who's-been-doing-anything-other-than-cheating routine. At the sound, she half turned and looked over her shoulder. "I didn't hear you come in." Her voice was about half an octave lower than he'd heard it in quite a while. She turned completely, slipping the robe from her shoulders as she did.

"Kristin," he said, "you're naked."

"Just like you wanted."

Their eyes met. Reflexively he looked away. Not down, as she would expect, but away. Recognizing a cheater's tell, he tore his eyes from the wall and back to hers. "Uh—pardon?"

She smiled. "Today. Your email. Don't be so shy. You haven't talked to me like that in a long time." She held his eyes. "I liked it."

Liked what, goddamn it. He only emailed her if he wanted her to pick up— Jesus. No. No.

"Oh, the email. Oh that." He tried to chuckle. Which he couldn't really do when a big blast of adrenaline had set every muscle spastic. His lips were twitching. As a result, the chuckle came out somewhere between a sob and a gargle.

She smiled. It was the nicest smile he'd seen in years. "Come on. It's just me after all." Christ, when had she decided to get all nurturing on him? "Look. You don't even have to push." She settled back on the couch and stretched out legs that suddenly seemed a lot longer than they used to. He hadn't seen her like this in daylight for a long time. Boy, she sure was blonde. Boy, it sure looked good. It looked even better when she folded her hands behind her head and thrust her breasts forward just enough to show him that they were being offered.

For just a moment he forgot where he'd been all day. He felt himself stir. Slowly. For an instant he wondered at his sluggishness. Then he remembered why. Three orgasms in an hour and a half earlier that afternoon. Suddenly a glacial advance became a headlong retreat. Oh shit. In an instant, every last fatal possibility burst from the back to the front of his mind. Rug burns on his knees. Hickeys on his abdomen. The usual gusher just a dribble. Smelling like another woman from head to toe.

Just brazen it out. It'll come back. He crossed the Kilim rug to the couch in a stumbling sprint and fell on his waiting wife, trying to cover his panic with passion.

It didn't work. "Honey, what's wrong?" She hadn't called him "Honey" in months. "I didn't mean to scare you. Hey, you're shaking."

Well, in a minute he was going to cry. Not trusting himself to answer he pawed away with hands that might as well have been meat hooks. She gently pushed him away. "Are you okay?"

"Uh, yeah, of course. I'm just really excited."

She slipped her hand between his legs. "You are?"

He sighed tremulously. "Yeah, well, and I guess a little nervous. I mean, you're right, I haven't talked to you like that in a long time." Inspiration struck. "I guess I was just taking a risk. I was scared." She was always a sucker for vulnerability.

Kristin was grave. "I know you were. I love you for it." She pulled his head closer and ran a tongue across his lower lip. "And it was very sexy." She guided his icy hand between her warm thighs.

It turned out okay, Frobisher thought as he sat stunned over pizza that night. Eventually he had pleaded an unusually strenuous workout to cover for the muscle obviously worked past exhaustion and dived into a one-sided oral session that had left him with a jaw that threatened to unhinge completely at any moment. Grueling workout it had been, he thought, as he gingerly chewed a sundried tomato. Even though Amber screamed filthy religious epithets in Spanish and pounded his chest so hard he thought she'd break a rib, that night Kristin slept naked for the first time that year. And he hated it.

He had to talk to Drake.

Drake on trial was hard to get. Eventually, though, he responded to the increasing frequency and urgency of Frobisher's calls. They met for dinner that Thursday night. Drake picked the restaurant. Way downtown. It made Frobisher a little uncomfortable. Borough accents, Armani suits, and missing digits. When Drake blew in fifteen minutes late all the guys who wheezed hello to him sounded as though someone had tried to garrote them in the recent past.

Frobisher winced when Drake ordered. "I can't believe you actually eat veal."

Drake rolled his eyes. "Christ. Listen, Mahatma, it's not as though they just clubbed it to death in the alley. Anyway, what the hell are you wearing on your feet? Looks like dead calf to me." Frobisher had a sudden image of Drake leaping onto an antelope's back and breaking its neck.

The waiter showed up with appetizers. "St. Francis here won't be having any prosciutto. Just melon." He broke off some bread. "So anyway. You look like you've had your head in the microwave or something. Like a piece of beef jerky. What's up?"

"Jesus. I wish you wouldn't put it that way." He told the story as quickly, and as quietly, as possible. None of the thugs at the neighboring tables looked like they were sensitive enough to have dysfunctional plumbing. He was sure that if he was overheard, they'd start nudging each other and laughing and making incomprehensible little Sicilian hand signs and laughing harder.

Drake stopped chewing halfway through. When Frobisher finished, he finally swallowed. "Let me get this straight. You think you're sending dirty email to Amber?"

"Right."

"Kristin gets it?"

"Right."

"Kristin gets all gooey?"

"Right"

"And you can't get it up?"

"God, would you please keep your voice down?" Frobisher almost blew a disk in his neck as he scanned his neighbors for a response. All remained nearly face down in big bowls of pasta and crustaceans.

"Hey, listen, kid, don't tell me that never happened before."

"Well, maybe a couple of times if I'd had about twenty tequilas—"

Drake snorted. "Right. Listen, when the jury was out in that wire fraud case and I was still seeing that big Swede from the perfume counter at Barney's—well, she did things that could get her sent to prison in Georgia and I couldn't manage al dente. Happens. Big deal."

Frobisher felt a little better. "Really?"

"Oh, come on."

"Well it couldn't have been a worse time."

"That I can see. How was it with Amber?"

"What do you mean?"

"Still trying to shoot pool with a rope. Sorry. You know what I mean."

"It was great with Amber. Just the same as it ever was."

"And with Kristin?"

"She's been working late so the opportunity hasn't happened. I'm a little scared to try. Actually, that's not the problem. The problem is that I don't know what to do about the whole situation."

"What whole situation?"

"Kristin and Amber. I mean, I started to see Amber because of the way things were with Kristin. And now maybe things could be better after all. And that's what I wanted. But now I don't want to give up Amber."

"Why?"

Frobisher struggled for words. No. Well, maybe yes. "Well, I have these feelings for her, too."

"I can imagine. Jesus, she must—"

Frobisher shook his head. The restaurant disappeared briefly as he imagined Amber nuzzling Drake's Caribbean-tanned hide. His face flushed with an anger as old as the species but new to him—it was *his* harem, dammit!

Modern man reasserted himself with some difficulty. "No. I mean I feel responsible. I can't just dump her. I'd feel like something out of Balzac or something."

Drake lifted an eyebrow. "Uh huh. Say, this is really good. You sure you don't want some?" He started to transfer some tender flesh onto a bread dish. "Oh. Right. Sorry. Yeah, I think this guy was named Ferdinand. Nice soft nose. I used to see him at the petting zoo. What's the matter with doing both?" He didn't quite smile.

"How could I?"

"What've you been doing?"

"I know, I know, but I also know I've been pushing my luck. Kristin's sure to find out."

Drake rolled his eyes again. "Kid, the smart money says Kristin knows anyway."

"What?"

"Smart lady. How smart do you really think *you* are? Do you know how tough it is to cover every base, twice a week, for a year? Can't be done. I make a nice living off guys who find out it can't be done. And these guys are professionals. And crime's a lot simpler than adultery."

Frobisher twitched. He hated the word. In fact, he hated just about every word associated with his present domestic situation. "I can't keep this up forever."

"Sounds like keeping it up is a bit of a problem, kid. Sorry. Just slipped out. But listen. Assume she knows. And Amber sure knows. She does know, doesn't she?" Frobisher nodded. "And she doesn't have any expectations?" Frobisher shook his head. A little too fast. Drake settled back in his chair and studied him from eyes heavy lidded. "Bullshit."

"Well she knows that I'm not—wasn't—happy with Kristin."

Drake sighed. But not without satisfaction. Frobisher guessed it was good to know that the whole human race followed the same set of rules, and that no exceptions were carved out for family, friends, or himself. "Nothing in writing?"

"Of course not."

"And nothing verbal in front of her friends? At dinner or a party or something like that?"

"I don't know any of her friends."

Drake studied him for a few seconds. "No. No, I don't think you would." He sipped espresso. "Listen. Remember this. Kristin knows. Don't rub her face in it. And whatever you do don't confess. You'll feel good, she'll feel awful, and there's no putting the cat back in the bag. She'll be thinking about it on your deathbed and on hers. So just keep on keeping on."

"But it feels so wrong."

Drake smiled his little iron smile and nodded sadly. "Sure. But what difference does that make? We want what we want. This big knot at the top of the spine? The one that thinks it's in charge? Just there to help us get what we want. Which is fed and laid. Speaking of which, I've taken care of the one, so. . ."

Then he was gone. Actually, not quite gone. He stopped on the way out to confer briefly with someone who looked like Jabba the Hut in a black suit. Leaving Frobisher with the tab.

That Saturday, Frobisher was afraid to get out of a purely architectural screen. God knew what was waiting for him out there in cyberspace. When he had come back to the office the previous Monday morning, he had frantically pulled down the Sent Mail menu in an effort to figure out how the hell Kristin had got something intended for Amber. It wasn't hard. This point and click stuff was great for those who didn't have anything to hide. But if wife and mistress have entries right below each other in the personal section of the address book, it's really important to watch the cursor. Because, as Frobisher sadly reflected, you should always keep your cursor where it belongs.

What the hell. Email them both. But let's err on the side of caution and only do Amber once this afternoon. He clicked Receive just to warm up.

Oh God. No. Not Kristin.

Darling—

Today when you get home, I want to do for you what you did for me last week.

And I know how you like it. First, I'm going to put that massage oil in the microwave—

He couldn't read any further. A year ago, he would have cracked the underside of his desk with the force of his response. Now he just felt guilty and a little bit embarrassed. She really was trying, wasn't she? Maybe he hadn't been fair. Maybe he should give Amber a miss that afternoon.

Speaking of which, she'd been a busy little beaver herself.

Hey stud!

What's happenin? Three o clock thats what! Thats when the Fman gives his Amber—

Oh God. What was he thinking about? For twelve solid months he'd been jeopardizing his marriage and betraying someone who loved, trusted, and respected him—for what? For some fly girl who couldn't spellcheck. But who *could* make him whimper like a puppy with a few flicks of her tongue in the right places.

He sat at his curvilinear workstation, hunched in his Aeron chair, head in his hands. As he ran his fingers over his scalp, through one of Bumble and Bumble's more sensitive creations, Drake's words echoed. *We want what we want.*

Well, he thought. Here I am. Frobisher, lab rat. Chasing that food pellet. Battering himself bloody as he bounces off the walls of the maze. Wanting what he wanted.

He straightened up and stared at the screen. Which now displayed only his wallpaper. Piero della Francesco's "Ideal City." A fifteenth century vision of the Platonic absolutes in stone and mortar. Buildings stately as Euclidean wedding cakes bordering a piazza. Empty. Empty, Frobisher knew, because only the good, the just, and the beautiful could have lived in the presence of such austere splendor. People made the best they could be by the buildings in which they lived. Perfect people in a perfect city. Not one of them cheating on his wife.

After a while he made up his mind. Fuck Drake anyway. What the hell did he know? He'd been hanging off his every word like some kind of idiot teenager listening to war stories at a gas station. Drake was just an aging roué teetering on the precipice of absurdity. And how great could his life be anyway? He was never anyplace but the courthouse, his office, the gym, or a restaurant. His apartment was a closet for fifty suits. And the three successive dirty weekends that Drake called a relationship only impressed the idiots at the gas station.

So don't listen to him, said Frobisher to himself. Trust your instincts. Do the right thing. Live up to the best rather than down to the worst.

He squared his shoulders. First Amber.

His ears were still ringing when he got onto the four oh seven. He also had what could well have been the beginnings of a black eye. Probably not. But just maybe. She hadn't caught him square.

It had been much, much worse than he feared. What he expected was a sad parting of the ways. Okay, maybe some recriminations, half-spoken but clear enough to hurt. Well, he was man enough to take it. Or as he actually put it to himself, a big enough person to accept responsibility.

That's how he had begun. Grave and sorrowful. It was wrong of him to get involved with her while he was still married. He owed it to her to leave her alone as long as he was still with his wife. Thus, he broke it off while artfully leaving open the possibility of a reunion down the road. Down deep he thought that if Kristin's new leaf turned out to be anything short of the whole tree he could drop back into the old life. But at least he'd be able to say he'd given it his best shot.

Amber hadn't taken it well. No, not well at all. Unfortunately, he'd been a little less scrupulous about raising expectations than he'd led Drake to believe, even if Drake hadn't believed him. It had never really occurred to him that the things he said in the postcoital afterglow could be held against him. Anyway, he didn't remember those things all that well.

Amber did. At first, she sat there looking a lot like Thumper in the high beams of a Peterbilt. Her mouth tightened. Here it comes, he thought. She's going to cry.

"Motherfucker. Mo-ther-*fucker*. You were gonna kick that cold bitch's ass out to the curb? Right. *Motherfucker*. You loved me. Right. You loved my *pussy*, motherfucker. You think about it up there in Westport. You remember it. And remember this. Motherfucker."

It was clumsy and he saw it coming. But Frobisher hadn't been in a fight since Watergate and he'd never been hit by a woman. So, he just kept his hands in his pockets and barely turned his head. It hurt more than he thought it would. For an instant he thought that after this terrible catharsis she'd really finally start crying and he could leave on the moral high ground.

No such luck. After the first swing connected, she overbalanced a little bit and almost fell. That didn't help her temper. "Motherfucker." Frobisher backed up two paces. Those nails never looked dangerous before. They sure did now. His jacket was on the couch. Let it stay there. He could always get another. He thought he'd heard her breathing hard before. Not like this. She was standing there with nostrils flared and eyes like swordpoints. Don't take your eyes off her. And whatever you do don't turn your back.

Doorknob. Doorknob. Right here. Thank you, God.

He slammed it shut behind him and stood there with both hands in a death grip on the knob. Please please please don't let it turn. He had a horrified mental image of her pursuing him down West Broadway. Then he had an even worse image of her cornering him in the stairwell. He wasn't sure who'd win a fair fight. If she didn't try to leave right away, he'd know she was sobbing or throwing pillows and he'd have at least a few minutes to get to a subway stop that wasn't the obvious one a block away.

It had been a full minute without attempted movement from

the knob. Good. Or without sound from within. Maybe not so good. Maybe she was just waiting to spring. As quietly as possible he made his way down the stairwell.

For a little while he considered the possibility of reforming his life in stages. This afternoon hadn't been easy. But some stirring of self-knowledge assured him that if he didn't maintain confessional momentum he'd slump back into his moral torpor.

Maybe he could set a tone. When he got to Grand Central, he stopped at the florist. Another guy was just ahead of him. They eyed each other with the kind of curious disquietude usually reserved for adjoining urinals.

The other guy looked at Frobisher and then looked back fast. "Holy shit."

Still stunned, Frobisher didn't respond immediately. "Uh. . . pardon?"

"Jesus," said the other guy. "She should be getting *you* flowers." He laughed and shook his head. "Try ice." He picked his parcel off the counter and stuck it under his arm. "I thought I had it tough."

Christ, thought Frobisher as he gingerly felt his face. It was swollen. And hot. He took his dozen long-stemmed reds and bought a cup of ice at Zaro's.

Now Kristin.

There was a smell in the air that he couldn't place at first. Oleaginous and warm.

He knew he'd smelled it before but hadn't smelled it in a while. Then it struck him in the brainstem with the kind of short-circuit force that comes only with visceral memories: microwaved baby oil. Oh boy oh boy. During the few seconds he hovered in the doorway blood began to pump through face and hands and groin, dissolving guilt.

But only momentarily. He was a man on a mission. Kristin was wearing a different robe this time. His.

She saw the roses. She smiled. Not the way Amber would smile, all childlike glee and giggles and wet kisses dissolving into sweaty nakedness. A slow smile. Surprised. If you paid attention to the curve of lip and sudden damp flutter of the eyes you could see the symphonic interaction of sentiment and thought. It was as though Frobisher was seeing it for the first time. It was. But it had happened before. He just hadn't noticed.

So, he put the roses on the table. He told her. It didn't take long. Two minutes, tops. As he spoke, he realized that he'd dived off the high board and was going to hit the water whether he wanted to or not. He wanted to stop in midair and take it all back, to reverse his trajectory and make everything run backwards like a home movie until he was standing on the board again, grinning and secure, flexing muscles for the camera. But words, once released, are gravity's slaves and plummet as inexorably as any diver. Falling whether or not there's water in the pool.

Her da Vinci smile faded as slowly as it appeared. It didn't disappear altogether until his last lame line— "I love you, I'm sorry"— had hung in the air for a full thirty seconds. The combination sounded adolescent even to him. And he had just that instant realized that he was in a very adult situation.

Kristin nodded slowly. "So." Her mouth tightened just a little. Frobisher hoped she was struggling to control tears and that she would lose the fight. He knew that once she cried, he'd be okay. Not immediately perhaps. Not by Monday morning. But eventually.

"So." She looked him straight in the eye. Hers were alarmingly free of moisture. How was it that he'd chosen the purge himself on the one day in recorded history when no woman cried. "Interesting. Very interesting. I had no idea. How stupid am I."

"You know you're not stupid. You're the smartest woman I know. Smartest person," he added immediately.

She sniffed, not as a precursor to a sob, but dismissively. "Right. That's why we're having this conversation. Because I'm so smart. And because I was smart enough to marry a smart guy like you. Speaking of smart. How smart were you? I mean, with her."

"Kristin, I know it was stupid—"

She made a chopping motion with her hand. "That's not what I mean. I mean, were you safe?" His confusion must have been evident so she explained. "Did you use condoms?"

For a moment he was relieved. If she was this clinical maybe she wouldn't be that mad. Then the anxiety balled up in his stomach again, the same fear that had been driving him the previous twelve months. Lies, the truth, or somewhere in between? He decided to stick to the new policy. "No. I mean, when it first happened, it was kind of a surprise, so I didn't, you know, I wasn't, uh, prepared—"

"Shut up." Funny, she'd never said that to him before. Her mouth was a small straight line. "Great. You broke up our marriage and then tell me that maybe you've killed me. Nice work." She picked up the phone and hit a speed dial number. "Hi. This is Doctor Frobisher. I need some stat blood work. Two samples. One I'll run in. The other you pick up at the hospital. ER in an hour. Yeah. HIV. I'll fax you the permissions on

Monday. Thanks." She turned to him. Still no emotion. "I'll do my own sample here. You go to the hospital. I'll call in the order when you leave."

The reptile brain was in control again, this time with fear instead of lust. His palms and soles were wet. He always trusted Amber. What if he was wrong? "Why can't you do my sample?"

"Because I don't want to touch you." Her eyes were still dry. "I'm not going to touch you. Ever. You're not going to sleep here again. Ever." She blinked hard. Tears at last?

No. Just thinking. "I've changed my mind. I'm drawing my blood at the office. Get what you need for the next week or so and take it with you. Go to the hospital. They'll know what to do at the desk. Don't come back here until your lawyer has talked to my lawyer. I'm not going to see you again without a judge in front of us."

She picked up the roses. They were still in plastic. She wound up to swing them across his face but checked herself as he recoiled. Her arms relaxed. She smiled again. She held them out. "Take these back. You know I thought that these were the cruelest thing you could do. But I just realized you're too stupid for cruelty. Now go. Call my office for the results."

He hesitated. "By the way," she said. "Your eye. I guess your girlfriend—Tiffany?"

"Amber."

"Amber. Amber didn't like getting dumped very much. Ice and Ibuprofen. Now I mean it. Go."

He left.

Drake didn't find himself alone very often. That's why he liked his Saturday mornings in the office. Secretary and paralegal gone, no clients or witnesses, Dizzy Gillespie on the CD player, French roast from the shop downstairs—a moment of peace. Also, a time at which he could use his reading glasses without fear of discovery.

He was getting ready to go. First read the email. Well, what do you know? Frobisher. He hadn't heard from him since that brutal day judicial imprimatur was given to the capsizing of the marital ship. Ugh.

He had warned Frobisher going in that spilling to Kristin had put him in such a position that he'd need a proctologist more than a lawyer. Worse, the judge they drew was notorious for thinking that Hester Prynne got what she deserved. Not that there was much the court could have done if it wanted. Kristin earned about five times as much as her ex-spouse-elect and had ponied up the down payment for the baroque space station they called home. Drake argued for alimony and half the equity as compensation for the value of his architectural services. Compelling as these claims might have been, they wilted in the face of his opponent's rather expressive readings from Amber's deposition testimony. Issuing judgment from the bench the court had managed to work in the line, "You play, you pay." Through it all Kristin had sat there looking like Madame Defarge. Frobisher, on the other hand, trembled noticeably. Particularly when it became clear that he had to buy Kristin out of the house he had built.

The handwriting was then well and truly on the wall. Frobisher tried. Grant him that. Unfortunately, the market valued an architectural bauble differently from its architect. Lots differently. Frobisher defaulted on the brand-new jumbo mortgage after a few months. His nonexistent equity presently became the property of the bankruptcy trustee. Shortly thereafter he stopped calling and Drake was not surprised to learn through an announcement that he'd relocated. Big time.

Well, hell. Let's see what the kid has to say for himself. Drake pointed and clicked.

Dear Drake—

I'm sorry I dropped off the face of the earth like that. Maybe Fort Wayne isn't completely off the face of the earth, but it's sure a long way from Nolita. I'm sure you understand I just had to get out of town after what happened.

The house was bad enough. The bankruptcy was worse. I'm sure you heard about what happened with me and the firm. I guess I got sloppy because I was so distracted.

I guess that shouldn't surprise me. Maybe I've beaten myself up enough. But what did surprise me was Stephanie and the others. I always thought we were friends. I really counted on them. I guess I shouldn't have been surprised that the hospital wasn't going to want us on that addition after what happened. I should have known that they wouldn't be all that interested in my side of the story.

So anyway, Fort Wayne isn't so bad. And it's a lot cheaper than the City.

Which is good because draftsmen don't make all that much. I'm renting a condo with a guy who works at the Post Office. It's actually not bad, but he has his kids on weekends, which I don't really enjoy.

*Is Amber still at the Apogee? I called her and emailed
her but she never got in touch.*

Anyway, I have to get back to work. Take care.

Drake read it through twice and then sat quite still. At length
he stirred. He pulled an Upmann from the Edwardian humidor
on his Deco desk and clipped it with practiced grace. He fired
up and swiveled to look down two stories to Greenwich and
Duane. A nice day. Lots of nice-looking people out.

He squinted through smoke at the screen. He had always
known that the kid wasn't smart enough to figure it out on his
own. He had hoped, though, that he was smart enough to listen.

But he wasn't. And there he was in a Midwestern trailer park.
Kristin was on a Prozac drip somewhere. And the bank had got
soaked on the house.

Oh well. He dropped his reading glasses into a drawer. The
same one that held the vial with the blue pills. Which he tossed
it into the gym bag beside his chair.

Amber would be waiting.

MY SUMMER VACATION

Boyos,

I hope you got through the Fourth better than I did. Every year for I don't know how long I did the same trick. Hold the bottle rocket warhead in the teeth, wait for wife to light the fuse, and then with an athletic toss of the head flip it spinning skywards just as it ignited. Quite a sight done right just at sunset.

This year, I don't know, I guess it was the heat. Had to be. See, it was nearly a hundred here in CT that day and like an asshole I ran at two in the afternoon—how odd, I thought, no one else seems to be on the streets—so I was pretty thirsty when I got down to my in-laws party in Westport at four and they had a quarter keg of Bud—I know, I know, you don't tend to think of kegs of Bud in Westport but remember Paul Newman lives there—and the party was outside so I started sucking it down pretty good there and I know I was dehydrated because when the sun was going down at nine, I still hadn't taken a leak.

Which is when I went out into the yard for my famous trick. My wife was saying, I can't believe you're still doing this, you're forty-five, and my brother-in-law was saying, hey Terry, it's okay, we have a satellite dish, we can watch something if we get bored, but I kept saying no no no, tradition's tradition, and anyway there were forty people or so in the yard clapping their hands and chanting RO-KET RO-KET.

So I was out in the yard and the rocket was in my teeth and my wife was taking so long to light it my saliva mixed with the gunpowder and it tasted really weird and I thought hell this might turn into a dud after all and all of a sudden sparks started flying and my wife ran back and the crowd cheered and I started the head toss and I don't know what happened then but I must have let go a little late so my head was facing straight up when I let the rocket go so that's just when the engine catches which meant it drove straight down through my open mouth into my alimentary canal.

I don't remember exactly what happened next which I guess is a blessing but they say there was dead silence when the rocket disappeared down my throat and then there was this muffled CRUMP when it blew up in my stomach. They say I stood there for nearly half a minute before I started clutching my throat and then my belly and then I started running towards the kids' inflatable wading pool and I guess I kind of pushed a couple of the kids out of the way a little harder than I should've but consider the circumstances so anyway that was what the EMTs pulled me out of, amazing how fast they got there but that's Westport for you; no crime, no welfare. I guess their taxes have to go for something.

So I just got out of the hospital. It's funny, but it turns out what they had to do for me to fix my stomach was just like that thing they do for the guys who get over five hundred pounds and have to order their bib overalls through the mail and shower after they shit because there just isn't enough paper, ever. Tonight, I had three peas for dinner.

ACTS OF CONTRITION

I saw his shadow fall.

I was looking away from the window, opposite it in fact, at the rectangle of light it cast on the fifties paneling and old theatrical posters on Sid's back wall. I was tired of looking at Sid, so I thought maybe I'd brush up on the big road productions of 1969, just in case it was ever a category on Jeopardy. Just in case I was ever on Jeopardy. As I was wondering whether the babe in the Oh! Calcutta! poster was a grandmother, the rectangle of light disappeared and reappeared. It was so fast I thought something was wrong with my contacts.

There wasn't. "Holy shit!" Sid usually had a pretty good two-pack-a-day rumble, but the last word came out a falsetto squeak. He was out of his chair and nose-flat against the window in the time it took me to snap my head around. No mean feat. Sid was the kind of big fat guy who runs dirty book shops but who happened through a lucky roll of the genetic dice to inherit what used to be a theatrical hotel. Now, except for the occasional thespian too unknown to rate better, most of its guests lived on disability.

He covered almost the entire window. His hands were on either side of the sill. "Jesus, Sid, what is it?" I said. "Boy or girl?"

He spun as fast as a fat guy could. "Didn't you see it? Didn't you *hear* it?"

"See what? Hear what?"

"Not much, asshole. Just some guy just went past my window at about a hundred miles an hour. Going down."

"Jesus Christ." I was on my feet now too. "You heard him?" We were both headed for the door.

"Kind of."

"Kind of? Was he screaming or something?"

"I heard him hit. He sounded like a water balloon."

"Jesus." We were through the lobby and onto the street. It was the middle of an October Tuesday morning. Not much traffic. Just the guys from the Korean grocery standing in front of the shop staring openmouthed and starting to wonder whether the approaching siren meant that the cousin in the back room was going to have a big INS problem.

I was a little bit relieved when I saw the body. I thought he'd look like roadkill without the treadmarks. Instead he was just a guy curled up on the sidewalk, maybe having a little snooze. For a moment I wondered whether he might still be alive. Then I noticed the puddle forming around his head. Then if you paid attention, you saw that he was spread out and flattened slightly on the pavement side. He must have been going pretty fast when he hit the concrete.

I figured it was the cops' job to look at his face. But Sid had to look, too. After all, it was his hotel. He swallowed hard, getting ready. "Hey," he said, "I hope the fucker is at least paid up for the week, huh?" He walked around to the other side to get a look. From the way his face changed I guessed it had to be pretty horrible. Maybe the guy's eyes had popped out or something. "Shit," said Sid. "Shit. Shit shit *shit*."

I didn't say anything. I didn't know what to say. Sid walked back around the body. The siren was getting louder. The cops would be here in a second.

Sid looked like he was thinking. "It's Holy Joe."

"Shit," I said. It seemed the only thing to say.

Holy Joe had been what is usually described as a loner who kept to himself in post-mass-shooting reportage. Luckily, that wasn't his claim to media attention. He lived with his mom and went to church every morning at St. Lucy's on Wooster Square. One day after mass he noticed that one of the peeling sycamore trees in the park looked just like Jesus. Pretty soon all the little old ladies in the congregation were seeing it too. By the weekend there were klieg lights, special duty cops, and a couple of thousand people goggling at the tree. The Virgin was spotted in the tree next door, and then Lucifer gnashing his teeth in another. The tabloids picked it up first and within a week it was on Japanese TV.

But that was two years ago. Joe had not dealt well with fame. Obviously.

Sid turned suddenly and bounded with his surprising new speed up the four steps to the lobby. I followed. I knew where he was going. Fortunately, the elevator was free. I didn't want to think what would happen if Sid tried to go up five floors by stair.

"Which room?" I asked.

"And what makes you think you're coming, asshole?"

"I'm the press, asshole."

He snorted. The elevator doors opened and he pulled a passkey out of his pocket. I knew we only had a couple of minutes before the cops came up and I wanted to see the place first. Sid was right; Holy Joe was a celebrity, and the wire services would pick up whatever I had to say and then some. Next week, I'd be out of features and maybe out of town. The word Pulitzer formed in my mind and I pushed past Sid and into the room.

Of course, the first thing that hit me was the open window. Cheap curtains with some kind of mock Colonial pattern flapped in the light breeze. But the breeze didn't do anything to cut the smell. Not the musty stink of a headcase SRO. It was a grandmother smell, powdery and warm and sweet.

Then I noticed the source. On the dresser were maybe a hundred votive candles, all lit, flickering in little glass jars the colors of hard candy, deep green and blue and red. They were arranged around all these statues of the Virgin. Some were little plaster jobs that looked like First Communion gifts; others, Baroque confections dripping gilt that I guessed had come from Holy Joe's fans in the glory days.

Every other flat surface in the room looked the same. If I closed the window, we would have suffocated in minutes. On the walls were the kind of pictures you see in Italian grandmothers' kitchens: highly colored representations of Last Suppers and Bleeding Hearts and Crowns of Thorns.

"Jesus," I said. "Jesus."

Behind me Sid guffawed. I surprised myself by getting angry. I mean, the guy had been dead about five minutes and he obviously took this stuff pretty seriously. But before I spoke, I saw what he was looking at.

In the center of the unmade bed was a pile of magazines. From where I stood, I could see a couple of titles: 'Big Black Titties,' 'Ebony Orgies,' and 'African Leather.' Well, he was consistent, give him that.

Sid, still laughing, was holding something in his hands. He extended it. "Recognize this?"

I didn't, really. The thing was about a foot across, elliptical, and mounded in the center. It was light pink except in the middle where it was almost magenta. It seemed to have a slit or cavity in the middle of the deepest pink. Something liquid glistened in the slit. "I don't."

"Jeez. Your social life must be worse than I thought. It's a pussy."

"What?"

"Okay, well, not a real pussy, obviously, an artificial pussy. And because I just found a switch back here, I can tell you it's an electrical vibrating artificial pussy." He fumbled with the back and the thing almost jumped out of his hands. "Whoa, down girl. And I hate to say this but it looks like it got kind of used in the past, oh, ten, fifteen minutes."

"Isn't that evidence?"

"Of what? You think it pushed him?"

I was still trying to absorb the notion of an artificial pussy when two cops walked in. I knew them both. I'm only a features writer but it's a one-paper town; we get to know everyone.

Quagliano was the first to speak. He was pushing fifty but still carried himself like some thirty-year-old cavone, paunchy but taut, with a forty-dollar haircut and I think a little bit of a tint going on. He said he wasn't a detective because he couldn't stand the paperwork. Which wasn't quite right. He wasn't a detective because he was stupid. "So hey, Sid," he said. "Not for nothing, but you got this dead guy in front of your place. And whaddaya know, here you are in his room with Jimmy Olson Cub Reporter."

"Hey Quag," I said, "showing your age. Jimmy Olson's in the senior center."

"Yeah right. Shut up." Good to see that the cops know and respect the power of a free press. "So Sid. Tell."

Sid passed the artificial pussy to Quags. "Well, Sherlock," he said, "I don't want to interfere in police work or anything, but here we go. One we got a religious nut who jumped out my fucking window. Two we got a room that looks like the fucking Vatican. Three we got a pile of Afro-American split beaver gazettes. Four we got a freshly-used artificial pussy. Five we know that these candles don't burn that long. So here's what I think. Holy Joe fucks this rubber snatch while studying these Somalians and then feels real bad about it, so he lights these candles, says some prayers, and jumps. Or maybe he lights the candles, fucks the rubber snatch, and then jumps. But the way I see it he's fucking a rubber snatch and jumping."

Quag's lip curled. "You know what? I didn't ask for your fucking theory."

"You didn't? Oh. Say, you know you got a dead guy's jizz all over your shirt?"

Quags looked for the first time at what Sid had handed him. Oddly enough, he didn't seem to have any trouble recognizing it. Nor did he have a problem identifying the viscous fluid that had run out of the orifice and onto his nice navy uniform. He flipped the fake pussy into the air like a midget pizza and ran out of the room.

I thought Sid was going to wet his pants or have a stroke or something. But Sid wasn't the only guy laughing. This surprised me. Mike-the-Cop is so called because he is the image of probity. He is also one of the scariest looking people I've ever seen. He is a five-foot-seven-inch two hundred pound African-American Pentecostalist with a shaved head who can bench press five hundred pounds. Three times. He looks like a mailbox. With a gun.

The doorway was suddenly busy. Quags was back and he wasn't alone. I was getting a little antsy. I wanted to get to a phone. Another hour and someone was calling it in to AP before me. But now I couldn't leave. Not with the mayor there.

The mayor always made me wonder whether there was an extra Stooge who didn't get through the screen test. He had rubbery lips and pop eyes and really bad hair. His presence, though, meant the story was as big as I thought.

His voice was particularly unfortunate, high and crackly, like a dolphin attempting human speech. "Sid," he said. "Nice. You let a saint snuff it."

Sid sounded genuinely aggrieved. I didn't blame him. "Hey, I'm running a hotel, not a clinic. I give these guys towels and sheets. Not Prozac. What the hell was I supposed to do?"

"Hotel? You call this fucking flop a hotel? Just because you got a couple of actors from the Rep staying here with the nutjobs? How many times I got to get between you and the state to keep you open? So you can make a couple bucks off a bunch of crazy peoples' disability checks."

"I keep 'em off the streets," said Sid.

"Oh yeah? You do? Well one of them is *on* the street right now, face down, asshole. Jesus, Sid. Maybe talk to the guy once a month or so when he paid his bill. Maybe show some interest. Maybe, I don't know, call somebody when he started to look like he was going off the deep end. Maybe remember you live in this town. And that you fucking owe me." The mayor's edgy whine was heading up into registers that were making every dog for blocks whimper and urinate. He turned to the guy with him. "Hey, Tommy, what's up with this guy's liquor license? He get it yet?"

Tommy-the-Thug was pretty close to the Bizzarro-World version of Mike-the-

Cop. He was a thirty-year-old fixer on the make who'd sold out to the Dark Side before he knew whether there was another side buying. "Pending," said Tommy.

"Good," said the mayor. "Forget about it, Sid. It's history. And that's just the appetizer." In another minute he would no longer be audible to humans at all. "This is going to make me look like an asshole. We got great ink out of Joe. Guest of honor at every right-to-life rally between here and Boston. and now what? Even without *this* guy we're on Rather tonight." He jerked his head at *this* guy, who happened to be me.

Quags coughed. "Uh, Nick." The mayor jerked upright and glared. "Sorry. Mr. Mayor. It's actually kind of a bigger problem than you think"

Sid cleared his throat and explained. In terms somewhat more delicate than those he'd used with Quags. So delicate, in fact, that at first I didn't think the mayor got it. Tommy sure did. He rolled his eyes, crossed himself, and ran his big Irish head into the wall. Twice.

The mayor nodded slowly. "Oh. Okay. So our most famous citizen not only takes a dive from our own little piece of the Bowery, he has one last little fling with a mail-order sex toy first. Oh. Oh yeah. Before I forget, he's face down in a centerfold of Miss Nigeria while he's pumping the latex. But not until he's turned the place into Saint Peter's Basilica. So it's not so bad. Maybe we could host the North American Man-Boy Love Association convention next year. And I can blow a Boy Scout to kick it off."

"Christ," said Sid. "What are you panicking for? How the fuck did you get yourself elected in the first place?"

"*What?*"

"You heard what I said. Now cross your legs so your tampon doesn't pop out. I'm telling you what we're going to do." He did. When he finished, the mayor didn't look nearly as angry as when he came in. He looked at me. "Okay. Okay. Tommy?" He glanced at the Thug, who nodded once. Then he looked back at me. "What about *this* asshole?"

I was *this* asshole. What a surprise. "I got a story to cover," I said. "Now maybe two stories."

Tommy laughed. This was always bad for someone. "Oh, right," he said. "What's this, Woodward, Whackoffgate?"

He was going to continue but the mayor stopped him. "Don't fuck around, Tom." He passed over his cell. "Call the rag. If they want the tax abatement for the new plant this story gets spiked and this guy covers Little League for the East Shore Shopper."

Tom flipped the phone open and started to punch buttons. Four digits in he stopped and raised both eyebrows. "Well? What's it gonna be, Bernstein?"

I thought hard. On the one hand was journalistic integrity and a shot at a big break. On the other was the certainty of a medium-sized break and the continued ability to pay for little luxuries like rent and day care. And I also thought about my wife's Italian grandmother reading this story in the morning, clutching her chest, and going face down in her biscotti. With my byline on the breakfast table.

I didn't have to think long. "Okay," I said. "The pussy isn't necessary."

The mayor and Quags laughed at the same time. "Hey, kid, it's always necessary for this guy," said Quags.

I ignored him. "So that's me," I said. "But if it gets out I ate this, I'm buried. What about *these* guys?"

"What guys?" The mayor looked perplexed. It obviously hadn't occurred to him that the Civil Service Commission and a couple of unions could kind of get in his way with the uniforms. "These guys? Come one. Hey, Quags, you want to retire a lieutenant or a sergeant?"

Quags was not a big thinker, and he never tried to act like one. "Lieutenant," he said.

"Attaboy." The mayor turned to Mike-the-Cop. My stomach clenched. The mayor's multicultural sensitivity was not all it could be. I was afraid he was about to offer Mike two quarts of malt liquor and all the Popeyes he could eat.

I was close. "So," said the mayor. "You forget what you saw and you go to the top of the extra-duty list downtown. What's hard about that?"

Mike's face was impassive. I remembered all of a sudden that he was a deacon. "I don't think so," he said.

"What the fuck?" The mayor looked at Tom. Tom didn't do anything.

"I saw what I saw. I'm on the job. It goes into the report." His face hadn't changed. His eyes looked like obsidian chips.

"Hey Mike." Sid's voice was softer than I'd ever heard it. "Whatever else this guy was, he was a man of God. Let people remember him that way."

Nobody moved. At length, Mike spoke. "Okay. I didn't see

it." He turned to the mayor. "Forget the extra duty. I'll take my turn like everyone else." He walked out.

"Okay, assholes," said Sid in his normal voice. "Let me do the talking downstairs too. But first, Scoop, you call in the story. We'll listen."

By the time we walked out of the lobby, Joe was in a big bag on a gurney and there were a couple of TV trucks making absolutely sure that the crowd knew that this was a big deal.

The mayor, of course, couldn't leave all the talking to Sid. Not with gubernatorial aspirations and an uplink to the networks. He kept it short, though. A tragic accident had cut short the life of a man many considered a saint. As was about to be explained by one of our city's businessmen: Holy Joe's friend as well as his landlord.

I was impressed. Microphones, cameras, and what was by now a couple of hundred people left Sid unfazed. "I've known Joe for two years," he said, "ever since he saw the Holy Family in Columbus Park and came here to have a little quiet. And he was a quiet man, so it was hard to get to know him at first. But I saw him every day and we would talk and sometimes we would pray together."

Incredibly, Sid got this out without turning into a pillar of salt. This was not what he'd mentioned upstairs. The mayor's solemn face didn't twitch, but his eyes seemed to bug out a little more, which I wouldn't have thought possible without them actually leaving his head and bouncing down the steps. Tommy-the-Thug was a little less restrained. Checking first to make sure that the cops on the steps below shielded his body from view, he dropped his fist to crotch level and made a few quick jerking-off motions.

Sid had seen his shot and he wasn't wasting it. "In the last few weeks he told me that he had seen something over the Green, in the clouds. Just when it was cloudy, like it is today. You can see the Green from Joe's window, but you have to lean out and crane your head to get a good view. I guess today he leaned too far." He paused as though overcome. "What he saw was the Blessed Virgin Mary. I guess he's with Her now." Then with one big hairy paw he made the Sign of the Cross.

I actually heard a few muffled sobs. Sid stood with his head bowed and then turned majestically back to face the hotel. He lifted his eyes to the fifth floor where Holy Joe's curtains billowed and flapped in the breeze. Then he turned again towards the Green. His big moon face scanned the clouds like a satellite dish. So did every other face in the crowd. I saw the Cross made a dozen times. A cop reached into his uniform shirt to extract a crucifix to kiss. I picked out details from murmurs that rose and fell like surf. "Holy Mother of God." "Madrone."

Sid started up the steps. We followed. Just as we got to the door Tommy-the-Thug leaned over and whispered to Sid just loud enough for me to hear. "You're a thief and a whore," he said, "and I admire you for it."

I didn't know about Italians until I met Gina.

I grew up in the Iron Range of Minnesota and went to college in Madison, Wisconsin which my folks pretty much considered Sodom and Gomorrah because there were two gyros joints on the same street and you'd see hairy girls in Birkenstocks holding hands in the food co-op. But the Olive Garden was pretty much the only toehold the Italian Boot had dug into the shores of Lake Mendota.

After I got my first real job and moved east, I remained oblivious to the depth and breadth of the cultural divide. At least for a couple of weeks. But it hit me the first time I went out with the boys from the newsroom on a Friday before Christmas. We went to an upscale gin mill with wood paneling and yards of beer and Ivy League oars suspended from a smoke-browned tin ceiling. Happy hour wound up ending about nine o'clock. While we stood on the pavement outside laughing men wrapped their arms around one another and kissed cheeks and wished "Buon Natale," I stood rigid and sweating . As one advanced towards me my editor grabbed his shoulder and said, "He's not a hugger." No, I'm not, I thought, as I shook hands as warmly as I could.

I had been in town less than a year and sunk pretty much all of my discretionary income into a gym membership. I was pumping away on a bike when she walked past in a jogbra. I first noticed the cleavage and then I saw the crucifix. Jesus looked like an Acapulco cliff-diver, arms outstretched, ready to plunge into depths I could barely fathom. And that of course was the whole story, though I couldn't know it then.

So we started dating and then after a while she wanted me to meet the family. Sunday dinner. The whole family. Having met some of the key players individually in the previous few weeks, I knew that they had not, shall we say, completely dissolved into the melting pot. I also had the distinct sense that they'd never met a Lutheran before and weren't too crazy about this Reformation business anyway. So I decided hey, when in Rome, so to speak. So I went out to the Barnes and Noble and got some cassettes and practiced in the car for a week.

I obviously hadn't really been paying attention to where I

lived because when she said 'the whole family' I thought she meant the mother, the father, and both siblings. You know, nuclear. Like the Cleavers. Did you ever see Beaver have an aunt or an uncle or a cousin? Do you know how many cousins you have? No? Right.

So I could hear them when I got onto the porch. And it was January so that meant they were blasting through a lot of insulation. Maybe there was some mistake. Gina opened the door. Shit. Right house.

There may have been forty people there. The guys were watching football and yelling at each other. The noise was so deafening and so apparently random that I couldn't begin to make out team loyalties so I decided to keep my mouth shut. The women were all in the kitchen whaling away at big aluminum foil trays.

Gina took me around to make introductions and I had the sense to just smile and bob my head and shake when appropriate. Her father treated me with his usual suspicious disdain. Until today I hadn't seen the tattoo snaking up his forearm. I was surprised when her mother kissed me. *My* mother doesn't kiss me.

The meal itself went reasonably well. I passed dishes and nodded and smiled whenever anyone spoke even though the background din made it impossible to pick out anything more than syllables. Gina looked at me every so often and smiled and squeezed my hand but I could see a little bit of that Bambi-in-the-headlights look of sudden despair. I wasn't fitting in.

Then I saw my big break. There was a tray of olives in front of her grandmother, the father's mother, an eighty-year-old widow with a face out of Leonardo's notebooks. I leaned over and asked for the tray in my best Barnes and Noble Italian.

She looked at me as though I'd just farted. Her mouth worked like a freshly hooked carp. She glanced at her son, Gina's father. Her son looked at her. Conversation stopped all around the table and probably all over the block. He leaned across the table. "What did you say?"

Obviously, my accent was a bit off. I repeated myself, clearer this time, my Tuscan crisp as breadsticks. "*PASSI PREGO LE OLIVE.*" My shirt was starting to stick to my back.

Around the table uncles were beginning to mutter. Jesus, what had I said? "Say it in English," said father.

"I just asked her to please pass the olives."

His lips moved for a minute. Just beginning to smile he turned to his mother and repeated the Italian I thought I had spoken, only pronouncing it as though he had a cleft palate and a mouthful of marbles. Grandmother's eyes narrowed, then widened as she let out an explosive whoop of laughter. Now that she had everyone's attention, she repeated what her son had said, in that weird Sicilian stroke-victim slur, then, pointing at me, repeated what I had said in an exaggerated mince that made me sound like a Neapolitan Oscar Wilde.

Nothing in the noise before prepared me for the hurricane that knocked me back in my chair. Uncles were pounding each other on the back; aunts wiped streaming eyes with their napkins; little cousins almost incontinent. Through it all Gina kept shouting, "He's trying! At least he's trying!" I knew then that I had no choice but to marry her. Obviously, a small wedding; nobody from her side was going to show up.

At last they stopped. Her father turned to me again. "Hey," he said, with something like tolerance. "Where the hell did you learn that? Switzerland? Okay, paisan, let's try it again."

It lasted half an hour. With uncles and aunts pitching in and grandma so delighted I thought she'd break into a tarantella. But when it was over, I asked for the olives in a garbled Mediterranean slur that actually got me the olives and a fresh glass of wine and a dozen claps on the back and a big handshake from dad. After that I wasn't in—I never would be—but I enjoyed the same respect and affection usually reserved for a diligent and mildly retarded bagger at the Stop-and-Shop.

So after that Gina and I got engaged and by and large it was smooth sailing. Not as smooth as it could have been, of course. Where I come from we don't really have tempers. Scores don't really get settled; no, they fester and metastasize and nobody really knows that somebody's mad until Oly's had about fifteen beers with brandy bumps at the Garrison Keillor Bar and Grill and all of a sudden he's swinging a barstool and the town constable's calling the States.

Here's how I learned about tempers. One day, before we were married, I looked at my watch and it was about a quarter to twelve and I knew Gina was home and I didn't have anything to do until two. So I went over and later we were lying there and she said, "Oh God, I could relish in this forever."

"Revel in," I said.

"What?"

"Revel in," I said sleepily. "You say that all the time. You either 'revel in' something or you 'relish' something. You don't 'relish in' something."

Silence. Then: "So I embarrass you?"

"For Christ's sake. No. I was just pointing something out."

She sat bolt upright. "So I've been wrong all this time when

I say I'm relishing in something? And you've said, oh, that's stupid guinea Gina, let's humor her so I can get into her pants?"

"Gina, look, I just thought—"

She threw the sweaty sheets aside and leaped to her feet. She planted her fists on either hip and thrust out her jaw. She looked like Mussolini declaring war on Ethiopia. That is, if Mussolini had a pair of solid D's and legs up to his armpits. "Oh, let's see if stupid Gina can use this in a sentence? Here goes. 'Let's see you *relish* a nooner again.' Wait, how about this: 'You won't *revel in* your dick in my mouth.'"

I was sitting up at this point and mouthing apologies. She tore the sheets away. "You come to my fucking house and tell me I'm a fucking idiot?"

"That's not—"

"*The fuck it wasn't!*"

Well, suffice it to say that thirty seconds later I was hopping one-footed into my Dockers and less than a minute after that I was in the parking lot buttoning my shirt and trying to open the door of the Tercel while she leaned out the window screaming, "Oh, how I *relish* this sight! Even a stunad like me can *revel in* a smart guy with no shoes! Oh, did you forget something? Here they are!"

She leaned out farther and wound up like she was throwing out a guy at first base. I was relieved to see that she'd pulled on a tee shirt; even in the middle of this bad Sophia Loren movie I didn't want the neighbors to see those gongs flapping around in an early spring breeze. Anyway, the first one—the right, I think—bounced harmlessly against the pavement. Her next, better aimed, ricocheted off the car's roof and caught me on the ear.

I turned speechlessly to the open window. She stood there in obvious satisfaction, her hands on her hips again. She nodded twice, hard, which sent everything jiggling. "I am *disgusted*," she said. Without another word she slammed the window shut.

The next day, of course, she was fine. Terrified, I had been unable to sleep the night before. I tried to bring up the scene when we spoke on the phone but all she said was, "What?" and in a rare moment of common sense I didn't pursue it. But I was having lunch with my editor that day, who was a) a woman; and b) Italian, or at least half. So I decided to ask her what had just happened.

"Easy," she said. "It's a contract."

"What?"

"Listen, Sparky," she said, "you've seen "The Godfather," right?"

"Right."

"And being a newspaper guy and all, you read about Sicilians blowing up Prime Ministers? By the way, is she Sicilian?"

"All four grandparents."

"Yikes," she said, spearing a ball of buffalo mozzarella. Which, by the way, in this town we call 'moots' in Sicilian fashion.

"So it's easy," she said. "Look, you ever wonder how it is that the folks back in the old country can do these terrible things and then build churches to the Virgin?"

"Yes," I said. "I just thought it was hypocrisy."

"No such thing," she said, chewing contentedly. "Contract. See, over there, when you do something to someone, steal his goat, invade his territory, whatever, you do that knowing that there's going to be a payback. *You know.* So when the other guy pays you back, blows up your car, whatever, he's just closing the deal. Nothing wrong. You knew it was coming. You knew it was coming when you stole his goat. You *consented*. So after he kills you he can go to your funeral and take communion with a clear conscience because hey, you knew you had it coming."

"My God," I said.

"So my advice to you, my friend," she said, pushing me the bread basket, "is don't piss her off. Or when you do, do it knowing that there will be a payback. And like they say, payback's a bitch."

It started the day of the funeral. I was feeling pretty good. The wire story had made page three of half the nationals. The Times wanted a piece for Sunday. All of a sudden, I was getting calls from agents who were thinking in terms of magazine pieces and maybe a book. It was working out okay. No Pulitzer, maybe, but I'd be a lot better off than just paying for day care.

So I splurged and paid two bucks for a recently-invented traditional European-type coffee and spun around the corner to Sid's place. In front of the hotel, on the sidewalk, at Holy Joe's ground zero was a mound of flowers nearly three feet high. Any day now there'd be a fountain. It was actually kind of nice to see that none seemed to have been disturbed. Probably bad karma, or its Mediterranean equivalent, to fuck with it.

Here was something out of the ordinary. There were about twenty little old Italian ladies on their knees on the steps of Sid's hotel. They were all saying the Rosary. I knew they were Italian because they were in uniform: black dresses and orthopedic shoes. They had considerately formed up in a double rank so that pedestrian traffic could pass. Just as I got to the door, I saw that the head cheerleader was actually a nun, of the old school, wimple pulled so tight that the flesh of her face popped from its starched confines. Kneeling, her head just reached above my waist. Thus, she looked exactly like a big penguin.

Once inside, I went straight to Sid's office. "Hey, monsignor," I said. "What the fuck?"

"What do you mean 'what the fuck?'"

"What's the deal with all the crows on the front steps."

"Oh. Them. Don't you love them?"

"Yes. Do you?"

"Fuck yes. Yes. They give me money." He laughed with childish glee. He was still wearing his funeral suit. He must have bought it five years and thirty pounds ago. Double-breasteds always look a little odd when you can't button the jacket, particularly when it's about a fifty short. Nevertheless, he had looked pretty good at Joe's funeral. He was three rows back, almost head of state seating when the Cardinal's officiating and the pallbearers are Kleagles or Grand Wizards or whatever the Knights of Columbus call their big guys.

"They give you money? Can't be because they like you. Nobody likes you except maybe me, and I think tolerance is about as warm as even I get."

"Tolerate this." He fumbled at himself in a hapless effort to grab his crotch, but he was sitting down, and his belly and thighs got in his way. "Fuck it. Anyway. The nonnies want to see Joe's room. So I show them. I told them that I'm very busy this time of year and it's very hard to keep the room vacant because of demand."

"On your best day you're maybe forty per cent occupied."

"Do they know this? So I tell them I'll hold out as long as I can. So they start pressing money into my hands when they leave. So I won't rent it out. They pray. They cry a little. They try to steal things."

"They *do*?"

"The madonnas. They can't resist. I've had to start asking them to leave their handbags outside the room. So I think maybe I might start up a little trade in artifacts. In fact, I already have. I got two hundred for one of the little ones. And you know those fucking candles? Twenty each"

I was impressed. But I saw a couple of flies in the ointment. "Uh, Sid. Those things aren't, uh, *yours* now, strictly speaking, now are they? I mean, I know his mom lives out in the Cove. They're hers, right?"

Sid snorted. "She was here yesterday with that little pious guinea lawyer of hers. She snuffles and rubs her beads. So I ask her to leave the room for a minute and the lawyer starts to read me the riot act about private property and unjust enrichment and shit. So I say hey, weren't you kind of running Joe's books for him after he got all that dough from magazines and TV and Steven Forbes and whoever? So he says, yeah, and? So I say jeez, isn't it funny that he wound up bouncing a couple checks for a hundred a week rent. Your trust account, too. I wonder where all the dough went. So he looks at me a minute and Mom walks in. He tells her everything is fine but that I'll be taking care of winding up his affairs here and it looked like he owed a few bills and some of the stuff would have to go. So that I'd be sending her whatever was left. Have a nice day, peace be with you, out they go."

"Nice." So that was where the money went. Why wasn't I

surprised. "But how much cake can you get out of this? Only so many candles and BVM's up there."

"Way ahead of you. Look." He pulled open a desk drawer. I went around the desk a little cautiously. Sid always had some pretty weird stuff in that desk. Some of it you could go to jail over just for knowing what it was, much less owning it.

In the drawer were maybe a dozen boxes. Their fronts were clear plastic so the contents were easily visible. Each contained ten blue and white statuettes of the Blessed Virgin. Behind the boxes were smaller containers full of votive candles.

"Jesus," I said.

"Exactly." Sid's grin was never pretty. "Exactly. A miracle. Loaves and fishes, asshole."

It was two weeks before I saw him again. I was sitting on a bench opposite St. Lucy's on Columbus Square eating a meatball grinder from Big Tony's around the corner. Three tour busses pulled up in front of me. All with Jersey plates.

The doors hissed open and people started to roll out. They were mostly middle aged or older, mostly women in scarves with the occasional husband in a VFW windbreaker. They were all looking in the same direction across the park.

"HELLO! WELCOME! GOD BLESS YOU!" A vastly amplified voice boomed across the square and broke down into feedback squeals and eventually silence. I could see a figure in the middle of the park bending over a big black box that I took to be some kind of amp. The figure straightened up and waved to the busses. It looked something like a bear with a hormonal disorder. I recognized it immediately and joined the crowd, now moving towards him.

Sid was wearing a headset. He finally had the amp under control. "Thank you for coming. God bless you for coming." He was wearing a dirty tan raincoat, open like an exhibitionist's, under which I saw a clerical-looking black turtleneck and a big pectoral cross. "We're standing at the foot of Joe's Tree." A hundred heads craned towards the branches. "This is where his visions started. But this is a vision we can share." He whipped out a silvery tube that for a moment looked to me like a vibrator for an android. He clicked it on and a brilliant red point appeared on the tree's scaling bark. My God. Laser. Sharper Image. Who'd have thought?

"You can see the nails through Our Savior's feet where I'm pointing." The light danced up and swung right to left along adjoining branches. "There they are through His hands." The light traveled up the trunk to an old bird's nest. "And there's the Crown of Thorns. It's harder for us now to see what Joe saw. But many times when we walked together Joe brought me here to show me what he saw. Some of you were here three years ago when Our Savior showed Himself to Joe and He was easier to see." A dozen people half-lifted their hands, tentatively, as though they hoped to be called on to witness but were afraid of calling too much attention to themselves.

There was a little old lady in black tagging along with the crowd. Obviously local; she was carrying a shopping bag from which I could see protruding a bunch of broccoli di rapa. Because little old Italian ladies are pretty much interchangeable, I didn't recognize her until she smiled and waved. Gina's grandmother.

Because her head was about four-and-a-half feet above the ground, I had to bend over for the big one-armed hug. "Nonny,"

I said, "what are you doing here?"

"I just want to see the tree again. Here every night when it happen. We didn't know you then. We all could come." She was certain that if she just acted as though I was a nice Italian boy, I would become one. Hey, who knows; she'd scored midnight mass two Christmases in a row. "Did you see it then?"

"Nonny, I came. But I couldn't see it."

She sighed and patted my cheek. Maybe sympathy; maybe a slap she just didn't have the energy to deliver. "You see it. One day I know. My Gina says you're a good boy."

I smiled and thanked her. I wanted to leave, but Sid was starting in on the Rosary. Gina's grandmother fumbled in her purse for the beads and started to creak down arthritically into the turf. I always hated it when this happened. I never knew what to do. I couldn't just walk off with her stuck in the mud. And anyway, I knew whatever I did would get back to Gina. The wrong move meant sleeping on the other side of a yard of cold sheet. So I stood there as Nonnie started the rhythmic mumble.

Suddenly I realized that I was the last man standing. This was the part I hated the most. When I did it in church with the whole family; then it was just good manners. Now it looked too much like belief. Oh hell; no way out.

My knees hit sod. Naturally I found a puddle. Gap cords aren't waterproof. And even Catholics don't really know how long a Rosary is supposed to last so they just keep going until exhausted. Halfway through it Nonnie put her hand on my arm for just a second. She squeezed and went back to her beads.

When the last soul was finally out of purgatory we got up. The busses started to fill. "You know this man with the hotel?" she asked.

"I do. He's—" Well, what was the word?"He's my friend."

"Can I see it?"

"See what, Nonny?"

"The hotel. They go back there now."

I was sitting in Sid's office a couple of hours later. He was just finishing up with the tour. I wasn't surprised about the trip to Joe's room, now permanently unoccupied behind a velvet rope and illuminated only by regularly-refreshed votive candles. Nor by the T-shirts and Joe mugs in the lobby at tour's end. And even Sid's suggestion that some original relics were available to bona fide religious organizations interested in contributing to the expenses of Joe's House was okay with me. I balked, though, when he showed them a pattern of mildew on the wall of the basement laundry room and related how Joe said it was a time-line predicting the re-establishment of Palestine, Monica Lewinsky, and Armageddon. And when Gina's grandmother wanted a Holy Joe rosary, I shelled out the forty bucks for her and got her into a cab before she could endow a chapel. So I went to wait in his office.

He looked tired but happy. "Hey Hootie. Like the goatee."

"You do?" It was only ten days old.

"Yeah. But it kind of makes your mouth look like an asshole with teeth."

"Speaking of which, how much did you clip these goombas for?"

"Ten a head to me for the tour and maybe a grand in sales."

"So about two large just for today."

"Two large for this afternoon. I got another tonight."

"No shit. Aren't you taking this a little bit over the top? I mean, with the time line and everything? Christ, what's next, JFK speaking through the ice machine?"

Sid laughed. "Wait. Slow down, slow down. I want to take notes."

"I'm serious, Sid. You're about to step on your own dick."

"I am? Hey, I guess it can happen when it drags on the ground."

"Just because you got two-inch legs." Neither of us was laughing. "I mean it. My editor is asking why I'm not doing any pieces on this circus. You don't want any more attention. You won't get any from the cops or the State's attorney. But the postal inspectors and the IRS don't give a fuck about the mayor. And I got to tell you I heard the archdiocese is getting a little embarrassed about this."

"Since when was I supposed to give a shit about them?"

"Smart. Very smart. You're absolutely right. The Catholic Church has no power in this state. And hell, even if it did, just because this is probably the most Italian state in the country, fuck 'em. Man of principal, Sid. Attaboy."

"Fuck you." He dropped into his desk chair. "Listen. Don't break balls. Another six weeks like this and I let the bank take this place and I go to Florida."

"Dunno, Sid. I think you got to stop sooner than that. You got to stop clipping these poor old people."

"Who says 'got to?'"

"I say 'got to.'"

He laughed. "Feeling mighty ballsy, sonny boy. I can see the big piece in the rag right now. 'Hotel Owner Fucks Old Guineas' Or something like that. Or 'scuse me, *you* see the big piece in the rag. But you don't see the sidebar. 'Rag reporter resigns in disgrace over eighty-sixed story.'"

"Huh?"

"Huh? *Huh?*" he mocked. "Hey, Safire, that's pretty poetic. Words your business or something?" He snorted. "Jeez, you sounded so much better when you were calling me a fuckhead. Listen. Connect the fucking dots. You don't like what I'm doing? Okay. Don't like it. Be my guest. But you think about doing something about it, you remember the day when Joe hit the dirt and you couldn't wait to bend over for the mayor. So you not only don't give me shit, you make sure I don't get shit or at least let me know if shit's coming. And I don't get hammered. Because if I get hammered, I tell the whole story. Which includes you *eating* a story."

I thought about it. He had me. "I can't protect you from everybody."

"Sonny boy, I'd be surprised if you could protect me from *anybody.* Now get your skinny ass out of here."

As I turned to go, I noticed something on the windowsill. The same one Joe had traveled past at such high speeds a month before. It was a little Virgin statue, unpainted plaster, nicked and chipped. I recognized it from Joe's room. Sid probably didn't want to give it shelf space now.

"Hey," I said, pointing. "That for sale?"

"No."

"Too ugly?"

"No. It's mine."

"What?"

"Joe's mom gave it to him for his first communion. I keep it for luck." Sid looked embarrassed. I hadn't thought him capable of it

"Right. Hang onto it, fat man."

The shop around the corner was still inventing traditional European coffees. I had one. If this was what they drank in

France for breakfast it pretty much explained World War II. I got an American drip and thought. The place had a pay phone for its few customers still too backwards or broke for cellular. I used it.

"Can I speak to Tommy-the-Thug?"

"Who?"

"Tommy."

"Oh."

A couple of clicks and the great man himself got on. "Scoop. What are you taking up my time for? Interview? Twenty Questions to the Kingmaker? Make it fast."

"Do something about Sid."

"Why? What's Sid doing that I need to do something about?"

"He's ripping people off."

"Big fucking deal" he snorted. "You do that whenever you deposit a paycheck. So what?"

"So you do something. Or I will."

"Oh. Right. I keep forgetting. You went to journalism school or something. Listen. Two words. Artificial pussy. Two more words. Hands tied. Capeesh?"

"It wasn't newsworthy."

As usual, the laugh wasn't pretty, but this time I think he actually thought something was funny. "Turn on the TV, asshole. Do you see *anything* newsworthy? Fuck, man, you would've been on Geraldo for a week. But you ate it. So don't give me this 'or else' shit."

I thought about it for a second. I'd thought about it anyway, but it was worth thinking about again. "Yeah. Yeah, I guess you're right. Tell you what. I'll hang up and then I'll call in and quit."

The laugh was now without humor. It was just tired. "Right. Good. Yeah, do that. And then call me back and tell me you did it and I'll call the rag and if you did do it then maybe you'll scare me."

"Nope. Next call I make is the Times."

There was silence for a full minute. "You'd do that?"

"Yep."

"Yep? *Yep?* Who the fuck do you think you are, Jimmy Stewart?" He paused. "Okay. Any point in just calling him?"

"What do you think?"

"Right. Listen, this won't be pretty. Or subtle."

"That's why I called you"

"Thanks, asshole. Let me call you back. What's your cell?"

"I'm at a payphone. I left my cellphone at home."

"Jesus, you *are* a loser. Can you hang there for twenty minutes or should I just leave a message at the shelter?"

I had another American drip. It was good. The phone rang in fifteen minutes. "Okay," said Tommy. "It happens tomorrow morning. Hey. Are you asshole enough to cover it?"

I hadn't thought of that. "No. I'll get someone else there."

Tommy laughed. "Twenty bucks says you don't have the balls to watch."

Tommy was usually right but not always. It was cold the next morning but sunny, so I took advantage of my new friends at the coffee shop and sat at one of their two sidewalk tables watching traffic. When an unmarked cop car went past, I got up and moved over to the Korean grocery across the street from the hotel. Two gold shields in plain clothes got out of the unmarked. Detectives are about as easy to spot as their cars; Crown Vics with whip antennas and city plates, and the cops dressed like plumbers at a funeral.

They went into the hotel. Five minutes later two Saturns with Federal plates pulled into a loading zone. Four guys with plastic briefcases went into the building. I waited for a long time. I realized very late that I'd left the coffee shop with one of their nice ceramic mugs. With all the cops around this made me feel very nervous.

It was half an hour before Sid came out. He saw the guy from the paper just in time to do what I hoped he wouldn't. He pulled his coat over his head as the camera started clicking.

It was time to go. I didn't want him to see me. Anyway, I had to get my mug back to the coffee shop before they missed it.

I didn't know what the deal was until after it had been cut. Sid squeezed the Mayor, the Mayor squeezed the Governor, the Governor squeezed both Senators, and both Senators squeezed the US Attorney. Criminal charges were dropped but half his assets went to the Government. The other half went to charity, which, oddly enough, turned out to be Catholic Family Services. The hotel got turned into a homeless shelter and the actors had to stay at the Holiday Inn like everyone else.

It was about six weeks after the dust settled. I was at Big Tony's again. It was too cold to eat outside. I was sitting in the window watching the beginning of a late November snow squall. I finished my egg and pepper grinder and went outside.

It was completely still and the sky was a featureless leaden gray that seemed about fifteen feet above my head. Snow was falling in sparse heavy flakes the size of saucers. You could actually hear them land.

Sid was the only other person in the park. He was sitting on a bench facing Joe's Tree. He didn't seem to hear me approach, and he didn't move when I sat down beside him. He was looking up into the branches. "So, Sid," I said. "Tell."

He didn't speak for a while. He had lost weight. He was still fat, but he'd shrunk to within normal limits. It was the first time I'd actually been able to see a face rather than separate features adrift in a sea of flesh. Finally, he turned to me.

"He was right. Jesus is here." He turned away and didn't speak any more. I glanced down. In his right hand was a rosary. In the left was the Virgin I'd seen in his office.

I looked up. Still just a tree.

It was a few weeks later. I had the graveyard shift so it was still dark when I had breakfast at Big Tony's. I heard the sirens and looked up curiously. Little Tony was the only other guy there. Behind the grill. Big Tony only came in those days to talk about Omaha Beach and Powerball. I was going to go to the window to see what was up but Little Tony was already on his way. If it was important enough to interrupt sausage and cheese on a hard roll, he'd tell me.

"Jesus," said Little Tony. I decided my aorta could go another couple of minutes without another coat of protective plaque. I went out onto the sidewalk with him. I wished I'd remembered my coat. Even with global warming, dawn during Christmas Week in Connecticut can be pretty cold. Little Tony was colder, with nothing but a greasy apron and a Harley T-shirt and the tattoos.

The square was right in front of us, hundred-year-old trees even leafless protecting its interior from the graying sky. St. Lucy's, on our left, was bathed in floodlights, as it always is during the festive season. Three NHPD cruisers were pulled up on the little fake Neapolitan piazza in front of it, barricading the statue of its patron saint as though she might stick her eyeballs back into her head and walk off with the poorbox.

"What the fuck?" I said through the gummy remnants clotting my mouth.

"Over there. Jesus tree." Little Tony pointed towards the peeling sycamore at the center of the park, even now decorated with a couple of sorry bouquets at its base. And now decorated with a little bit more. There were half a dozen cops there, clustered around what looked like a walrus and a big broken treelimb. The cops were milling around with tape measures and digital cameras and walkie-talkies. One of them looked up into the tree and then looked down and shook his head. Another made the sign of the cross.

"Looks like some asshole hung himself," said Little Tony. He made the Sign and spat on the ground. "Christmas a week away, too. Thank God no kids saw this, huh? Not for nothing but this ain't Santa down the chimney, know what I'm saying?"

"Right," I said. "Hey, maybe I better take a look."

"Right," he said, smiling sourly. "Story."

"Yeah," I said. "Hey, my job."

As I was heading into the park on one of its long diagonal walkways a fourth cruiser pulled up with a very stylish squeal of rubber. Behind it an ambulance that just plain parked. Obviously, no hurry. The ambulance guys lumbered out and rolled out the gurney, careful not to spill their Dunkin Donuts three-sugars-and-cream larges. From the cop car swaggered what looked like a mailbox with a pro-league bowling ball on top.

"Hey Mike," I yelled.

Mike-the-Cop nodded once, sharply, and gave me a negligent salute. The salute made me go all warm inside. I was one of the boys.

We met about ten yards from the Tree. From where we stood, I could see the bottom half of the stiff, its top shielded by the tree's wide trunk. Big body. Obviously, a fat guy. Explained why the branch snapped. Maybe he wasn't dead; maybe he just tried to hang himself and the branch snapped and hit him on the head and knocked him out and he'd revive and it'd be the greatest Christmas Miracle story of the decade, maybe the century, like an O. Henry tearjerker.

But judging from the way the cops were snapping pictures and milling around they were pretty sure this guy was done. And from where we stood, I could see his hands, which were swollen to the size of outfielder's gloves and clenched into the fists of rigor with the deep grayish purple of early permanent death.

"So," I said to Mike. "Merry Christmas."

"Same to you, Scoop," he said solemnly. "Sorry about this."

"Yeah," I said. "Tough thing for the neighborhood."

"Yeah," he said. "You too"

"Why?" I asked. "Good luck I was here."

He snapped his head away from the crime scene and back at me. "That's all you can say? I thought you were friends."

"What? Friends with—" I looked back at the crime scene. Now an official crime scene, blocked off with yellow official cop tape cornered on adjoining trees. Big fat body. Big fat hands; even allowing for the edema of asphyxiation they were big hands when alive. Cheap Rockport knockoff shoes. Cheap brown polyester pants. Dirty beige raincoat. All in all, the kind of look you usually see on a guy who runs a dirty bookstore. Instead of a theatrical hotel.

"Oh," I said. "I get it."

"You didn't know?"

"Just got it," I said.

I must have been quiet for a while. "You all right?" Mike asked.

"Fine," I said. "This is my business, after all." I started forward.

A great big black hand wrapped itself around my little white bicep. "Don't," he said. "He strangled. You don't want to see."

I looked at his hand and then met his eyes. "Yes," I said, "I do."

He held on for a long time. Then he let go. "Okay, Scoop." I started to walk. "Pray for him. I will." I nodded but I didn't turn around.

So I kind of strolled around to the other side of the tree where the cops and the EMTs were very busy with their tape and the cameras and the coffee. To the right of the stiff, tethered to it by something thicker than clothesline, hairy and abrasive, was a tree limb easily twenty feet long, a big thing two feet thick at its raw fractured base and split into a dozen branches.

Left of the stiff was a folding chair. Maybe ten feet away. Lying on its side. About ten feet up the tree was a big white scar where a branch had been. Oozing sap. Slowly, given the season, but oozing nevertheless.

So I'd looked everywhere but at the stiff so I guessed it was time to look at it. And suddenly *it* was *him*. Like they say in the business, the corpse had a familiar face. He was wearing that same dirty raincoat and black clerical looking turtleneck he'd had on when I saw him at the base of this same tree with a laser pointer and a busload of credulous guineas. Only now his big fat face was even fatter, swollen above the cord almost buried in the folds of his swollen neck, purple as the eggplant that Little Tony would be slicing up for lunchtime grinders in a couple of hours. His eyes were half-open but showed only the bloodshot whites. The worst was his tongue, reddish black, hanging almost to his chin and nearly severed by his jaws' last spasm.

"Wow, Sid," I said, and I turned away and started to stumble towards the sidewalk when a couple of cops moved forward and said 'scuse me and bent over the corpse and started to pry the big hands open and then I had to run to one of the big blue plastic sand barrels to empty my stomach of half of a Big Tony cholesterol booster.

Mike was standing next to the stiff when I got back. Another cop was talking to him. Deferentially. I hadn't noticed Mike's new stripes. "Hey, Sarge," I said.

"Hey," he said. To the beat cop he added, "He's okay."

"Okay," said the beat cop. "So like I said, so he's still stiff, so it's like two hours, maybe three hours ago. So he stands on this little chair and he throws the rope over the limb and he ties it off with this little boy scout slip knot and he kicks the chair out. But it's not such a big limb and you can see he's a pretty big fat guy, or he was a pretty big fat guy, whatever, so the branch bends and his toes are just touching the ground, which is why the grass is all tore up there." I looked at where the cop was pointing it and did kind of look like a mad bull had been ripping up the turf. "So I guess he just kind of hung there bouncing up and down till he kind of strangled. You can tell his neck ain't broken. Not like you could, falling two feet with that knot and that neck, you know? Anyway, only thing is this, guy strangles and all you kind of expect he's gonna grab the rope with both hands and claw and everything when the lights are going out, right? I mean, no matter how much you wanna go, when you're goin' you wanna stay, right? Same with this guy, only not. Left hand, nails broke, blood all over his palms, like he's fighting for dear life, like your usual guy who hangs himself.

"So here's the thing. Right hand, it's clean. Nails like they was manicured. So we pull the hand open, and it takes two of us, which is a lot even for this big guy who's dead and all, and inside his hand which he didn't use to fight the rope, we find this.'

He handed something to Mike, who looked at it. "I dunno," said the beat cop.

Mike handed the thing to me. It was a little statue of the Virgin. Holy Joe's.

"So whaddaya think, Sarge?" said the beat cop.

"What do you think?" said Mike-the-Cop to me.

"I think," I said, "you should give it back to him. I think he made a deal"

"Drug deal?" said the beat cop.

Neither of us said anything. I turned the Virgin in my hand. Sid's right hand, the clean one, looked empty. I bent forward and put the little First Communion memento in his paw and folded his thick fingers around it. They were the coldest things I'd ever touched. Even colder than his eyelids when I reached over his half-severed tongue to slide them down. "No," I said, "not a drug deal. Just a deal. One way or another, you get paid back."

"So this is payback?" said the beat cop. "So who paid him back? How'd they get some big guy like this up on a chair?"

"He got up himself," said Mike. "He paid it back himself."

The EMTs had finished their coffee. The gurney wheels squealed on the sidewalk and were soon muffled in the turf as they dragged it towards their destination. I turned away as Mike and the beat cop helped them heave the body up.

I really wanted another cup of coffee. No, I didn't; I wanted three beers and a shot of bourbon and my wife snoring beside me while our son gurgled in his crib.

Mike-the-Cop was standing next to me. "Payback," he said.

"Payback," I said.

The sun was coming up. Late, I thought, but it was the shortest day of the year. Sid was sliding into the back of the ambulance and I saw a couple of the neighbors wandering over to Big Tony's. Mike and I watched the doors slam shut and the ambulance take off with an entirely unnecessary trill of siren.

We stood there a long time. "Well," said Mike, "Merry Christmas."

We shook hands. Mike went back to his cruiser. The sun was finally up. I went home.

THE THING THAT MATTERED

Hem didn't want to throw up. Not now. Not in front of Havana's top drawer. Not at this grave.

But he was close. His head was pounding. The sour taste of vomit was at the back of his throat. Breathe slow. He didn't want it in the mouth. He didn't want to think of the black licorice he ate as a kid. He didn't want to think about the absinthe last night.

It almost had him there. It took a sharp deep breath, but he stopped it. He stood there a minute feeling the sweat trickle from his armpits and down the stiff bulge of flank and belly that made him so sick to look at. Thinking about what he saw in the mirror every morning almost brought on the explosion again.

Christ, it was hot. It was the worst kind of tropical late morning, when you stand there in boiling sweet air, like a florist's shop with a ruptured radiator. And the mounds of flowers covering the grave didn't help. Any fool knew Rick wouldn't want flowers. But Rick didn't know many fools.

Rick wouldn't have wanted a priest, either. But there the priest was, fat as Hem but womanish, droning away in sad singsong Latin. And Rick wouldn't have wanted to be dead. Yet there he was, about two minutes away from dropping permanently into the wet Cuban ground on a hot Cuban day.

Hem tried not to look at the box. He tried not to think of the dead man inside and what he looked like right now. Rick had always looked good. Lots better than Hem though he wasn't that much younger and drank nearly as hard. Now he just looked like a dead man with half a head.

Hem had seen that kind of thing a lot during his war. Not the war he let his friends believe he fought in when they drank at La Floridita and he pretended that he had got to Paris before Eisenhower. The real war, the one before, the one where he drove an ambulance and saw a lot of brave men and men not so brave all coming to the same place, the place where the life is leaving them and they feel death spiraling in and they look in disbelief at the bowels looped around their hands and scarlet stumps flecked with shattered bone. That war.

They said he was too old when the last war started. But he was only forty-two. Men his age were getting drafted. Maybe too famous. But Rick was famous, too, in his way. But it hadn't kept him out of it. Out of anything.

They had known him in Ethiopia when the Italians and their tanks and machine guns and poison gas were losing a war against men who knew that you died just as dead whether you were killed by a lion or a bomb. But those men were grateful for the weapons Rick brought them so they could teach the Italians this great lesson. And they all knew him in Spain, where he ran guns to the Republicans. Hem heard that Franco said that every month Rick was alive cost him a battalion. That was when Hem had met him, when he was already too famous just to report the war and Rick had to watch where he was when he went out in daylight. And they knew him in North Africa, after he left Casablanca.

Hem heard too that Rick kept it up in Havana. He heard that the bars and the whorehouses weren't Rick's only businesses. He heard that some of the guns that went up into the hills came through the Cafe Americano and La Mariposa first. And he heard that Battista wasn't happy, and he heard yesterday that the reason Rick was going into the ground today was that Battista wasn't happy.

Pulleys creaked. The mounded flowers shook and the undertaker's men moved quickly to take them away. No point in burying them, too. Hem swayed slightly. Jesus, it was hot. Was it really hot or was it the damn hurt he got when he drank too much the night before? His sweat seemed different today, oily and thick. Maybe it was time to see that doctor. Maybe he was finally old. Maybe Rick was lucky. He had been spared this.

He looked across the open grave. He didn't want to watch Rick going in. Christ. There was Louie. Smiling his superior little frog smile. How the hell could he look like that? Suit crisp despite the heat. Body still slim despite the years. Though Hem was told he wore a girdle. And Hem heard that the girls you saw him with around town had to work harder and harder for less and less.

Louie looked up. He caught Hem's eye. His were red rimmed. As though he'd been crying. The frog smile was still in place. It just looked all of a sudden as though it didn't belong. Louie and Rick had been through a lot.

The priest was doing something with incense over the grave. Christ, when would this stop? Why the hell add one more stink to already overburdened air? Just then the first breeze of the day blew up. It pushed the priest's smoke towards him. Sweet and thick. It was too much. Hem's mouth filled with saliva. He turned and ran towards the bushes.

Louie caught up with him later. They walked in silence towards the cars. "This must be very hard for you," said Louie after a time.

"It is," said Hem. "He was a good man. Harder for you, I think."

"Thank you. But I'm afraid that's not quite what I meant. Forgive me, but I was referring to your Communist friends."

Silence again. Gravel crunched very loud under their feet. It was getting close to noon. It was much hotter but Hem felt better. Someone had had a flask with a little rum. "Do I have Communist friends?"

Louie laughed. "You have friends. This is Cuba. It's 1956. Of course you have Communist friends. More than you know I'm sure. But I'm also sure you have Communist friends you do know about. For example, two named Fidel and Che."

Hem remembered he didn't like Louie. He also remembered that Louie had worked for Vichy. So he didn't tell him to go to hell. "So we all have Communist friends. Why does that make today hard for me?"

"Papa, surely you jest. Why do you think we buried our friend just now?

"Only thing to do with a dead man." The headache was coming back now. Just at the base of his head. Soon it would take up the whole skull. Food would help. Hem started thinking about lunch. Prawns with his Habanero friends. Some beers. Maybe sleep in the afternoon. He hoped he could sleep again that night without liquor. He didn't want to feel this way tomorrow.

Louis laughed. "Well I do imagine you're right. You do know, though, Papa, that even the Cuban authorities are likely to bestir themselves at the violent death of a prominent American expatriate." He shook his head and whistled in obvious admiration. "And I thought I was corrupt when I was an authority myself. But these circumstances will penetrate even the deepest ineptitude and moral bankruptcy. Sorry. Don't mean to sound melodramatic. The funeral, I suppose. But do please remember that inquiries are being made even as we speak. Some of my friends tell me that Fidel and his friends are thought to be responsible." He was silent for a moment. He cocked his head at Hem like an attentive sparrow. "And you, Papa, are among those friends."

Hem stopped in mid-stride. "What the hell?"

Louis shrugged and smiled. "You knew, of course, that Rick couldn't break himself of his old habits. Why guns, I always asked him. You make a perfectly admirable living with gin and the roulette wheels and the girls, all of which are at least as interesting and much, much safer. Well. We see that I was right. I wish I hadn't been." The frog smile was fixed in place even if the voice quivered. "Forgive me. In any event, my friends tell me that Rick's friends—your friends—quarreled with him over price and availability. They appear to have thought that he was starving the People's Army or whatever they call it of the necessary wherewithal for the worker's paradise just to drive up the price. Thus an argument. It is thought that we buried the result."

Hem stood still. His clothes were sodden. He imagined

Louis could smell traces of liquor and vomit. "What's this about me?"

Hem thought he was right about the smell. Louis had backed up a step. "Papa, do remember that you are known by the company you keep."

"Maybe. But yesterday you told me that it was Battista behind it anyway."

Louis smiled. "He is, I am afraid, the usual suspect whenever anyone of wealth or prominence meets a violent end. But as exemplary a Caribbean politician he may be, even he can't be responsible for every well-attended funeral on this island. And now he has competition. Remember, Papa, the company you keep."

They were at the cars. Louis turned to a flowering vine and plucked a blossom. He slipped it into his buttonhole. Hem ground his teeth. Christ, was there no limit to the man?

Apparently not. A sleek Lincoln, late model by Cuban standards, rolled up. At the wheel was a mulatta who looked barely old enough to drive. "Papa, you'll let us drop you? Please, you look quite done in by grief." He followed Hemingway's eyes to the driver's seat. "Ah yes. Well. And to think I once told Rick that women might be scarce one day. Well they were. But that was North Africa and a long time ago. Please, Papa, let me help you in."

Hem had been at La Floridita for a long time when Laslo came in. He felt better. The big shrimp, heads and tails still on and hot from the oil, had hit the spot. So had the beers. He drank the first three very fast. He had been sipping for the past few hours. No more than three or four. Just six or seven in all then. If he took a nap soon, he would feel fine that night. Maybe just some wine with dinner and then a really good sleep. Tomorrow would be different.

They knew how to treat him at La Floridita. They greeted him like a hero and then they let him almost alone, just enough sidelong glances to let him know that they knew he was who he was. And if someone came in that looked like he should be recognized, everyone looked at Hem. They wanted to see how Hem would acknowledge the visitor so they would know how to act.

Laslo still walked as though he should be recognized. Funny. He hadn't got the message. Maybe he should have forgotten that little time he was a hero and remember instead that very long time he was hunted. Hem was surprised that he would forget.

But still he walked like a hero and at least some of the Habaneros recognized it. They looked at Hem to see what to do. Hem nodded at this man in his fine linen suit and big Panama hat and then nodded at the man sitting opposite him. The fellow at the table stood up and got the new man a chair. Hem would have jumped to his feet and embraced Laslo had it been earlier in the day. But even though it was only seven beers, it had been a tiring morning and he knew sometimes when he was tired like that there could be stories the next day. So he sat.

They shook across the table. "Victor."

"Papa. How was today?"

"Funeral. How could it be? Sorry you missed it."

"So am I. I just arrived. Trouble with passports." He smiled sourly. "I never had this problem until recently. That man from Wisconsin." Suddenly he laughed. "Actually, there was a time when I had even more trouble with passports. That man in Berlin."

Hem laughed too even though he didn't get it. Then he realized what man in Berlin Laslo meant and looked over his shoulder. "Still trouble with the Committee?"

Laslo shrugged. "It seems I always have trouble with committees." Hem wasn't surprised. The man didn't know how to trim his sails. Hem's lawyers told him he was safe but he was glad to be in a place where there could be no subpoenas. But if he wanted to go back to Idaho he didn't want to have problems because he drank with a man who could compare McCarthy to Hitler.

He decided not to hold his tongue. "Ilsa?"

Laslo shrugged again. "She won't be here." He sipped a beer as though it were cognac. "We lead our separate lives."

I'll bet you do, boy, thought Hem. I'll just bet you do, you stuffed shirt. Once when they were drunk, he asked Rick what she was like. "Pretty," said Rick.

"I know that," Hem said. "You know what I mean." Then Rick had looked at him for a long time. Hem started to sweat. He always felt that way when Rick looked at him too long, especially after he said something like that. Finally, Rick spoke. "She was like any woman. She was like one of the girls upstairs. Not as good, maybe." Then Rick poured more bourbon and didn't speak and didn't look at Hem for the rest of the night.

Hem looked at Laslo. "You know what happened?"

I got some telegrams. Someone shot him in the face."

Hem nodded. He didn't trust himself to speak. Was this eight or nine? "What do

you think?"

"What do the police think?"

Hem snorted. "They're Cuban. They think he's dead. They

think that because we buried him. Otherwise, they don't know."

Laslo considered. "He was shot in the face. He was in his office. There was no sign of a struggle or theft. That means he knew whoever shot him. And he trusted him." He thought again. "Or her."

"I guess you got a lot of telegrams." Hem was pleased he was following so well. The implication of the last words sank in. "One of the girls?"

Laslo shrugged. "Who knows? Was he with any of them regularly?"

Hem thought about Rick. He tried to talk to him about women. It never seemed to work. "He didn't talk about it much. He was quiet about women for such a ladies' man."

Laslo smiled. "My friend, that is probably how he stayed a ladies' man." Hem was starting to remember what he didn't like about Laslo. He was so damned European it made his teeth hurt.

"But as you see all I know is courtesy of Western Union. What do you hear?"

Hem's attention had wandered a little. A waiter took it as a signal and brought him his tenth. Maybe when he finished this he'd have just one of the special drinks they made for him here, the Papa Dobles, daiquiris with twice the usual rum. Just to be polite. But just one.

Hem made a big show of waving to a bunch of Habaneros who had come in and bellied up to the bar to crunch shrimp, tails and all, where he could see. These boys liked that, strutting in with boots gleaming from the second polish of the day. After this little delay Hem had gathered his thoughts enough to speak. "I hear lots of things," he said at last. "I hear that Battista had him killed because he sold guns to the Communists. I hear the

Communists had him killed because they thought he was jacking up the price."

Laslo considered again. He looked like he was used to thinking and liked it. "Papa, both things can't be true. Well, perhaps I speak too soon. I never thought Hitler and Stalin would sign a treaty."

"Didn't last long."

"Much longer than it takes to shoot a single American in the head. Perhaps they made a deal. Stranger things have happened." He lit a cigarette. "Who is your source, or better, who are your sources for all this news?"

"Louie."

Laslo laughed. Hem couldn't remember having actually heard the man laugh before. He was without humor. Prolonged consideration of history and the people's struggle had leached it from his bones and left irony in its place, the way a dinosaur's rotting flesh had been replaced with stone. A laugh seemed as out of place as a museum brontosaurus dropping its boney head and rooting for swamp cabbage a million years extinct. "Louie? Well, who better to tell both sides of the same story?"

Number ten was almost gone. Hem was feeling much better. Maybe a little rum with dinner. "What do you mean?"

Laslo took a silk square from his pocket and dabbed at his eyes. Maybe his fossil laughter hurt. "Papa, you're joking. Did you know Louie in Casablanca?" Hem shook his head. "He betrayed France for Vichy and Vichy for the main chance. I'm only surprised he didn't wait longer. Until he could see the Star-Spangled Banner on the horizon and the Germans burning documents, for example. But I digress."

Hem hoped for another beer. The man was forever on a soapbox.

"He's always played a double game. That is all I mean. No one could have a better opportunity to know both sides of a story."

Number eleven had arrived. The bar was full. Hem had to lean forward to make himself heard through the chatter and laughter and clink of glass. "That's not all you mean."

"That is all I said. That is all I mean." The square went back in the pocket. "I have friends here too. Other than yourself, of course. All, I'm afraid, on just one side. Perhaps that is why the Committee keeps asking to hear from me. Oh well. In any case my friends on that side tell me that Battista is starting to be concerned. He knows that there are guns in the hills. He wants there to be no guns in the hills. It is easier to kill a few people or a few dozen people in the city than a few thousand in the country."

"So Battista had him killed," said Hem. "But Battista didn't kill him. Neither did any of his men. Not in Rick's office. Not like that."

"No," said Laslo. "First of all, Rick wouldn't have been foolish enough to let one in that close. Second, they wouldn't have killed him that way. Too painless and private." Laslo swallowed hard. Perhaps he was thinking about different thugs in a different time. "No. Someone he knew and trusted. And I think we can rule out a purely private dispute. Rick didn't run his life that way."

Hem nodded. When you lived on the edge as long as Rick you didn't deal in shades of gray. There was only room for black and white, word kept or broken. Much of what Rick did was illegal, but Hem couldn't think of anything he'd done that was wrong.

Hem hadn't touched the beer in front of him. He was pleased with that. "So Battista bought someone close to him."

"Correct."

"So who close to him could be bought?"

"Well, Papa, not you. Even if you could be bought by anyone you have more money than you need. Sam never cared about money and he doesn't need it now. Anyway, is he even physically capable these days?"

"He hasn't sung for two years. He hasn't spoken for six months. He hasn't left the hospital for two. His throat is all cut away and he weighs eighty pounds."

"My God. Death mocks us, doesn't it?" He raised his eyebrows and pursed his lips and stared into the middle distance. "Louie has had a few financial problems, I'm told."

"You really are told quite a lot."

Laslo smiled sourly. "Well. If the FBI didn't let me have my mail I couldn't write back. Then no one would write to me. Then the FBI would have nothing to read." He lit another cigarette. "Your country is not quite what I expected. I write a lot. No one talks to me. Everyone is afraid. I wanted to march with the Negroes thinking that they at least had nothing to lose by association with me. But no. Apparently Marxism is contagious. And no one wants to invite scrutiny by Mr. Cohn. So, I read and I write. I was a little surprised they let me come here. Perhaps I shouldn't have. Perhaps you shouldn't be seen with me."

Hem put his hand on Laslo's shoulder and squeezed. "I'm scared of nothing." He was pretty sure he'd seen everyone in the bar before. "I'm scared of nothing." He had to have lunch with the Ambassador soon. Just to play it safe.

Laslo had been gone for hours. Hem sat and thought about what he had said. Sometimes he talked to his Cuban friends. Sometimes an American bought him a beer. They usually asked him to drink it with them. He had to be much drunker than he was to do that. When the sun went down he switched to rum. He drank this for a long time. Then Jose told him the car was here and he knew it was time to go because otherwise there would be stories.

He didn't stay long at the house. He sat and thought some more and took what he needed from the cabinet and slipped it into the waistband of his pants. He started to walk back towards town. It took him a while. It wasn't far; even ten years ago he could have done it in less than an hour. Even after an afternoon at La Floridita. But this night it took him more like two to get to the big house on the little side street.

The lights were on in the second floor. Hem knew they would be. The man who owned the house was never up before noon. He knocked hard. A mulatta girl, maybe the same one who had been at the wheel after the funeral, opened the door. She recognized him, even if he wasn't sure about her. Her English was bad so they spoke French. Of course. He was upstairs. Please follow.

Louie was seated in a plush leather chair behind a big mahogany desk that made him look even smaller and vainer than he was. He must have just come in. He was wearing a white dinner jacket and his bow tie was still knotted impeccably. In his lapel was the little red ribbon of the Legion of Honor. Well, he wasn't the first bastard to wear it.

"Papa. A pleasure unexpected." He twitched his sparrow head at the door and the mulatta left. The brass latch clicked. "A late night for us both, I see. Please. Do sit."

Hem stayed on his feet. Not without effort. It had been a long walk on a long day and he had drained a decanter before leaving the house. "No thanks. Son of a bitch." He was surprised at how easily the Luger came out of his waistband.

So was Louie. But just for an instant. "Papa. You have the advantage of me. In more ways than one. What do you mean?"

I mean I know what you did. You little frog queer son of a bitch."

"Queer? Queer?" Louie chuckled easily and leaned back in his chair, crossing his legs and smoothing the creases in his pants as he did. "I really think that's a bit much, don't you, Papa? Also a bit of the pot and the kettle. Except that I'm not the kettle."

"What?"

Louie tapped a cigarette out of a gold case. He leaned across the desk and extended it to Hem, an eyebrow cocked in polite inquiry. "No? I'm sure you don't mind if I do." He lit up and exhaled as luxuriously as any man who'd ever had a gun pointed at him. "Please do put that away. Or keep it if you feel like it. But you're not fooling anyone. At least here. In any respect."

Hem tried to speak but no words came out.

"Confused? Sorry. I do forget sometimes how much you drink. Too, too much, Papa. We must talk about that sometime. But not now. Well. I know a few things about you that you might find surprising." He took another long drag. As he let the smoke trickle out, he leaned back in his chair and crossed his legs. "First, I know that the gun is there for your comfort and nothing else. I know that you don't have the guts to kill a man. Not like this. Not in cold blood. Never did. Men like you never do. That explains all those animals you go to such trouble and inconvenience to go off to kill. All those bullfights and the chest beating and the lies you tell about the war. The first one, I mean.

"Second. I know exactly what brings you here. You think I killed Rick. I know that isn't true. I do know who did, and I know why.

"Which brings me to the third thing I know." He smiled. "I've known you how long, Papa? Ten years? I always wondered why you seemed to have such a mania for masculinity. At first I thought it was simply that you were an American from the middle of the country who drank too much and enjoyed his fame and started to believe his own lies. You remember I was a policeman, don't you? Even if I was a corrupt provincial policeman, I was still a French policeman. I asked my friends in Paris about you. Just out of curiosity. Always nice to know something about the great man about whom we orbit. Well. They told me things. You were very discreet when you were a young man in Paris, Papa. But still a few slip ups. An arrest or two in the public conveniences. A fight here and there with sailors that didn't have anything to do with them insulting your flag. Tsk. Who would have thought it?"

Hem's voice was choked but he got it out. "God damn it. That's shit. I was a married man."

"So were some of your little lavatory friends, I'd imagine." Louie ground out the cigarette and met Hem's eyes. "Papa. I don't care. I actually think it's rather sad to have to conduct affairs of the heart in a urinal. But. That's not what brings us here, is it? You think I killed Rick. I didn't. As I said, I know who, and I know why."

He cocked his head to the side. He was giving Hem his best profile, like Barrymore. "It wasn't cold blood that night, was it, Papa? I know you; you see. I saw the way you looked at Rick. I saw it ten years ago. That's why I made my little inquiries. Tell me, Papa, how did your heart declare itself that night? A kiss? A fumble between his legs? Or did you come to him dressed like a bride?" Head still tilted Louie laughed again.

He was right about everything except the thing that mattered. The bullet caught him just under the left cheekbone. Tumbling and mushrooming it tore off the top of his head. The impact knocked the chair back and over.

Though the room still rang from the shot Hem heard through it a sound from Idaho. It was the patter of heavy snow falling from pine branches at the first warmth of early spring. He stood quite still for a moment. As it faded, he recognized it for what it was, foamy fragments of airborne brain landing on desk and floor and wall.

Then he heard a sound he recognized from the war. He had heard it many times driving his ambulance. It was the wet crackle of bowels relaxing just past the moment of death.

The gun was quivering in his hand. He stuffed the Luger into his mouth. Still hot, the barrel burned his lips and he snatched it away. Not yet. Not this time. But soon. He had done the same with another gun, by then cold, the morning after Rick died, when he woke up choking in his own vomit, before he managed to convince himself that he'd had just another bad drunk dream. But then he had smelled the cordite stench of powderburn, on the back of his right hand, the smell that nightmares can't leave.

The mulatta was pounding at the door. In a second he would

go behind the desk because he had to, to put the gun into Louie's hand. He would tell Laslo how he had confronted the little bastard with the truth and how he hadn't been man enough to take his medicine. In a day or two they would stand beside another grave.

But that was not yet. Hem got to work. Soon he would not have to be afraid any more.

TOKENS OF AFFECTION

Rachel

He was late again. He was always late. I don't know why I put up with it.

I don't know why any of them did.

But I did. Once a week. Always Mory's.

I don't like Mory's. It has the kind of flavorless food that makes old Yankee men look so constipated. It has the kind of atmosphere that goes with it, stuffy and bloated. I feel like I'm eating in a museum. I hate the gummy tables with the carved names of long-dead freshmen embalmed in urethane. I hate the rich shrill wives. Even though it's not officially a men's club any more, every woman there who doesn't look like an undergraduate looks like she belongs to someone who belongs. Always a belonging, never there in her own right.

He belongs, of course. I always go as his guest. A waiter deferentially waves me to a table. We know he'll be late.

He was last week. My father had just died. I thought that for that, at least, he'd show up on time. Instead he was ten minutes late without even the usual negligent apology. In fact, he didn't even say hello. He just launched right in. "So I said to myself Christ, what the fuck am I going to say to her. And here you go and make it easy on me. Jesus, Rachel, I like that outfit. Very cool." I was wearing black tights and a big black turtleneck. "Wow. Mourning in Chelsea. Ha. Chelsea mourning. Where was the wake, Pastis? Listen, if I blow my brains out, come to the funeral like that and I guarantee they won't be able to get the coffin closed. Would you stand up and turn around? Come on, for me? Okay, not now. At the funeral. Promise." He tore open a pack of oyster crackers with his teeth. "Listen. I'm sorry. But I figured you must be pretty sick of sympathy. How's your mom?"

He got away with it. He always did. He was right. I *was* sick of it. When I found out my father was dying, I cried. When I found out that he'd chosen a gun in his mouth over another chemo session, I screamed so hard I sprained a muscle in my neck. Now I was tired of condolences that seemed awkward because I knew no one wanted to accidentally drop the S word.

So he was late again. I stared out the window until he bounced up. "Sorry. Judge on the phone." It was always something like that: a judge, or a doctor, or a witness. Or so he said. I think it was usually whoever he was trying to line up for the weekend. Though he said he'd mended his ways since Maggie.

He dived into the soup I knew to order for him. He ate as if the bowl said Fido on the side. Actually, he always reminded me of a dog. Maybe an Airedale in an Italian suit. He was about the same size. He had the same need for attention. I could imagine him jumping onto the table and barking if I ignored him.

"Listen," he said. "The weirdest thing happened to me this weekend."

"What a surprise. Look at who you live with."

"None of that, dammit. Anyway she's been doing much better."

"Great. So she's getting back to the baseline of just plain nuts."

"Yeah, well, I knew the job was dangerous when I took it. Hey, if you expect a sculptor to act like a CPA you have a rude awakening ahead, I can tell you." He started in on the fruit plate. If he had the table manners of a dog, he had the diet of an anorexic girl. "Anyway, I'm sitting in the office Saturday morning."

"Hey, cool story already. What an exciting lunch."

"Please shut up. Anyway, I'm sitting there and who blows in but Daphne. I guess she got confused between vacations and forgot what day it was. Or maybe she thought hey, I'm a partner in a law firm, maybe I'll go see what the office looks like. So she says I just saw Sarah around the corner having coffee with her father. And I think Christ, the bullet just grazed my ear. I was there half an hour before. I must've just missed her."

"Oh. That wouldn't have been pretty. When was the last time you spoke to her?"

"Eight, nine months, easy."

"And you left it how?"

"Call you tomorrow."

"Very nice. Great way to end. You went out with her for a year."

"Yeah, well, get out of my house, you crazy bitch never seemed to work. Even repeated weekly. So, I thought I'd try something a little less direct. Worked. Or so I thought." He paused significantly, waiting for encouragement. When I didn't indulge him he shrugged and went on anyway. "So after Daphne leaves I go out to my car. It was supposed to rain and I left the top down.

On the passenger seat I find a single red rose. Wrapped in paper. The kind you buy from a street person. So I think aha, Sarah must want bygones to be bygones. Then I find—" he rummaged dramatically in a side pocket "—this. Exhibit A. Right next to the rose."

The evidence in question was a square of newsprint, ragged edged, obviously torn from a paper. It was a cartoon from our arts, music, and personals weekly. The Screaming Man. Not the famous one that got turned into coasters and punching bags, but the product of a local artist, a picture of a guy with bulging eyes and distended veins and gaping mouth shrieking something that sounded like it came out of a Twelve Step program. Here the Man had a big hole in his chest with an anatomically correct heart lying on the table in front of him. He was on the phone. The boldface in the word balloon said *"Honey I know it sounds codependent and dysfunctional but this time I know it's love."*

His arms were folded. His terrier eyes didn't blink. "So what do you think?"

"Sarah did this?" It was meant to be a statement but it came out a question.

"I thought so. After all she was right around the corner. And she knows my office and my car. But it doesn't seem like her style. Too complicated."

"Maybe it was Maggie sending you some kind of romantic message." I tried to sound serious.

"Actually, that occurred to me. So, like a fool when I got home, I asked her. Jesus. Grand mal blowout. I thought I was going to have to stick a wooden spoon between her teeth. Not only was it not her, she was, shall we say, displeased that another should communicate with me in this fashion."

"What?"

"She didn't come out and say it, but she acted like she thought I was boning someone else."

"And?"

"And what?"

"Are you?'

"If I were, would I come home and voluntarily—unbidden, in fact—present evidence of something you would think I'd hide? Nope. Anyway, I'm a reformed character. Straight is the way and narrow the gait."

"After five months. A record."

He was never discreet about his girlfriends. At least with me. He said he wanted advice. What he wanted was an audience.

I'm not sure exactly how we had fallen into it. When I first started with his firm, he ignored me. I couldn't figure him out. His partners were old men or women with rich husbands. All waiting for five o'clock and Florida. This driven little dandy didn't seem to be with that program. When he finally asked me to carry his briefcases on trial, I understood why they tolerated him. He was very good. They must have thought the arrogance and eccentricity were worth it. We had our first lunch while a jury was out. Later we started to have coffee when the others were gone. He was funny. He listened. Soon I got invited to lunch again. When I left the firm it became an institution, once a week, always Mory's.

Sometimes it carried over into the evenings. We double dated. It never worked.

My husband was always out of his depth. I usually had to explain jokes to him as soon as we left the restaurant. It was even worse watching him with the girlfriends. They were always pretty, always sweet, and always wrong. Sometimes I would watch them watching him and wonder what they would do when they got home.

I had listened to him whine his way through four or five by now. No matter how melodramatically he complained, he always managed to extricate himself without consequences. Somehow, he always got away with it.

Him

Sometimes I think I'm a nut magnet. I draw mentally unstable women the same way a bug zapper draws mosquitoes. Actually, I think it may be the other way around. I'm the mosquito, saying hey, what's this bright glowing humming thing. Next thing you know, you're carbon. But if I haven't always gotten away clean, at least I've always gotten away. That's the important thing.

Then these things start showing up in the mail."Unfair"is a client word. But I found myself using it again and again. For once I was playing it straight; for once I meant everything I said. But this time, it was someone else fucking things up for me.

So, it's the Monday after I found the first rose. We're sitting in the kitchen. Maggie's looking better than she has for six weeks. A month earlier I'd finally persuaded her that what she was going through was no mere variant on artistic temperament. The occasion then had been coming home to find that she hadn't been able to get out of bed and had spent the day watching old movies with the sound off. To say that what she had gone through was an illness is like saying Moby Dick was one big damn fish; I had ridden it like Ahab tangled up in his harpoon lines.

So, we were in the kitchen. It was something of an event. This was the first time she'd cooked since the depression began. A big bowl of pasta and vegetables. She was looking good. Nothing you would call animated, particularly if you had known her before, but neither were her eyes fixed on the middle distance. I was especially happy that she seemed to have got over the rose-and-cartoon episode of the weekend. For an ugly day or so I wondered whether that was going to tip us over the brink again.

But apparently not. She had talked to someone about learning to weld so she could do this big installation piece she'd thought of. She didn't eat much of her pasta, but she did take out a pencil and start sketching on a napkin. She even laughed a few times, though I had to work for it.

With the plates still on the table I started going through the mail. Interleaved among second notices and no-annual-fee offers was a plain envelope, Hamden postmark, no return address. I slit it open and a xerox fell into my plate. I sponged off marinara with my napkin. Screaming Man. Identical to the one I'd received on Saturday.

She must have seen me twitch as I crumpled it. "What's that?" she said.

"Oh, nothing." How stupid can I be? You don't crumple up something and then say it's nothing; you say what it is. Unless you want to hide it. Nothing is always something.

Across the table, she looked like a death mask. Her features were rigid and eyes aimed straight at a spot right above my shoulder. "I want to see it." Her voice had that tone of exaggerated reasonableness that SWAT negotiators use right before they okay the tear gas.

This was not going to be pretty. But there was no point in

resistance. I smoothed it as flat as I could and without a word passed it across the table.

She studied it for a full minute. "Interesting. Very interesting. Who is she?"

"Who is who?"

"Whoever you're screwing on the side."

Of course, I've heard this before. But always with some basis in fact. Which makes it all the easier to deny; then I know which bases to cover, where suspicions could have grown, what anxieties can be mitigated with apparently sincere confessions of thoughtlessness. Here I had nothing to work with except absolute factual innocence. Always the worst defense.

"I'm not screwing anyone else on the side," I said. Clever. Eloquence, after all, is my business.

"Then who sent this? Who else knows where you live? Who else knows your car? Who else knows your office? Who else knows you work on Saturdays?"

Calm descended. "I can't answer the first question. My address is in the phone book. There may be fifty red TR3's in that condition on the East Coast; everyone knows it. My name is on a big sign in front of my office. Lots of lawyers work Saturdays."

"Be a lawyer in your office, then. Not here. You know what I mean." I did, of course. I was playing for time. I couldn't imagine what was happening. "Who sent this to you? Who sent it here? I think someone's jealous. And she's jealous because you're screwing her and she wants you to herself."

It was then that I felt that first pang of bitterness somewhere around my duodenum. Not fair. Not fair. Not fair. Three months after our first night depression had settled on her. It reminded me of Lent. Or better still Holy Saturday, when all the statues in church are covered with purple velvet in mourning, obscuring even the outlines of the figure beneath and the only light is the flicker of thousands of votive candles in their little glass jars. I lost sight of the vibrant character that had drawn and held me in the first instance. First sex went, then humor, then appetite. Though almost every synapse screamed for the ripcord, I chanced it. I hung in. I became a caretaker. My reasoning, which had absolutely nothing to do with what I did except to justify myself to friends and of course to myself, was as follows: Bimbos are a dime a dozen; artists aren't; therefore, it makes sense to invest in this. The unspoken and thus unrecognized predicate was, of course, a desire for permanency.

She had left the table. From the sound of things, she was changing CDs; from the sound of things, our next selection had to be beaten into submission before she could get it to play. She came back. "So, who is she?"

I had had time to think. "I'm not screwing anyone else. Don't ask again unless you really want to see me pissed. And you've never seen that. And you won't like it. Just think for one minute about what's been going on the past two months. Think about what I've been doing. Don't bother to apologize. Just think."

She did. She didn't bother to apologize. I hate it when people do what I say.

"Okay, so you're not. So who?"

"Obviously someone I used to go out with. Who else would do this I can't imagine. She must think it's funny."

'Which one, then?'

The ice was splintering beneath my feet but I kept on

tapdancing. Like everyone else, she was the model of maturity about her own exes; hey, what's past is past, what's a cup of coffee to catch up. But I've learned the hard way that once acquired, intimacy never quite goes away. And to press the metaphor, there's no ice to break. So, the point is once it's done, it's done. And more to the point no one's life gets any better if the incumbent knows about them. I never talk about them with her and I try never to even acknowledge their existence in her presence. Because I know that Hip Street runs one way. And not in my direction.

But this time I forgot. Maybe it was the second glass. "Which one?" I strolled down Memory Lane. Out loud. With a little too much detail and a certain nostalgia in my voice. Next thing you know doors were slamming. Needless to say, there was about a yard of cold sheet between us that night.

The next day there were three. Each identical to the others, each with a different postmark. The next day none. Same the day following. I didn't relax, but I started to think it might be over.

Wrong. Two in the mail and a fax from a Kinko's in western Mass.

I was beginning to get scared.

Everyone was suspect. I couldn't ask the girl at the desk at the gym for a second sweat towel without wondering whether she was spending her free time at the xerox. I wondered whether it had to be a woman at all. Recently a guy from the drama school had taken to following me around the weight room until I was driven to lacing my conversation with phrases like, "Jeez, aren't tits great?"

Lunch with Rachel rolled around.

"How's Maggie with all this?" she asked.

"About what you'd expect."

"Can't be that bad."

"Jesus," I sighed. "Give it a rest."

"You know it has to be Sarah."

"No, I don't." I said, pushing an unripened watermelon ball into a mound of low-fat curds.

"Who else then? Who'd you dump Sarah for, anyway? Coleen, right?"

"Right. Not her for sure. She benches more than I do. If she were this pissed she'd just deck me and I'd be afraid to get up again."

"The blonde from the phone company."

"No way. Didn't have the brains to lick the stamps, much less remember my address."

"Stephanie. The one who used to follow you around the gym clenching her fists.'

"Now engaged to some weasel. Stockbroker. Two and a half carats and a house on the water in Westport." I snorted. 'You really think she'd fuck that up to annoy me?"

"So, Sherlock,' she said. 'When you've eliminated the impossible. . . .'

I was silent.

"It has to be Sarah," she said.

"What did she ever do to you?"

"Nothing. So what? It's what *you* did to *her*. You've known it had to be her all along. You just don't want to face it." She finally picked up her turkey club.

"Shit. You're right, of course. I mean, what the hell can I do? Just call her up and say, 'Enough's enough?'"

"You could. You'd have to talk to her again. And she might be a little pissed."

"Jesus. I guess so. Well, I don't see any choice. But boy, I really really don't want to do this."

I didn't. Even though this particular crazy little episode had put me on the moral high ground, the amount of intellectual dishonesty it would take to justify my own conduct left me a little breathless.

I was still feeling tenuous when I got home. I'd taken to going back to the house after lunch to hide the mail. I didn't want Maggie to see it, and I couldn't just toss it. There was always the off chance the police would find it helpful after they'd zipped up our body bags. So I stuck it in my study. That night, Maggie found it. I thought she was about as far gone as she could get. I was wrong.

Maggie

All the little pricks cheat. All of them lie. All of them leave. The trick is to know this. The trick is not to let them have too much of you. Then they can't take too much away.

I thought this one was different. Then he started to get these things in the mail. They were copies of a cartoon he had found in his car. When that happened, he asked me if I had left it. "My God, why would I do something like that?"

He looked a little confused. "Oh, I don't know. Something romantic, I guess."

"Try passive-aggressive. This isn't someone who likes you. At least not in any way I'd like to be liked." I tried not to sound suspicious. His confusion looked genuine, but I had done a lot of hard work to trust a man again, and I could backslide the first time I saw his eyes wander.

I hated them showing up at the house. That was the worst part. It took away something I loved. It surprised me the first time I saw it; with his snappy suits and little car I thought he'd live in a high-tech condo with a rotating bed and underwater speakers in the bathtub. Instead it was a little cape he'd bought when he was married. That first time things between us were still perfectly innocent; I couldn't be sure whether we were dating or just making friends. I saw the old pictures and big gold damask couch and had a sudden sense that I could live there. Then I saw Aveda shampoo for redheads in the bathroom and I almost cried.

The bathroom was worse than the kitchen but better than the basement. The house kind of deteriorated as the space became less public. The living room and bedroom were all masculine and English-looking, with lots of wood and leather and gilded frames and books piled up in every corner. Everywhere you looked there was a dead king staring at you. His bed was so huge that I was sure that when he slept alone he must have looked like a bunny on a pool table. When you got to the kitchen you realized that the guy who lived there was after all just a regular guy who drank beer right out of the bottle and left the empties on the counter. Everything was Formica or linoleum and the appliances were twenty years old, and the ones he didn't use didn't work. He didn't even know how to use the oven. The bathroom was where the ghost of the first owner lived. The tile was turquoise. It was amazing. It looked like fiestaware. I loved it.

That first time in the house I wondered if he would kiss me.

He didn't. The next day he did. I gathered the courage to hear an answer I didn't want and asked him about the shampoo. I expected to hear that it was none of my business, and I swore to myself that this time if it wasn't my business, I wasn't going to be any of his. Instead he surprised me by looking embarrassed and a little sad. "Loose end," he said. "I didn't know for sure what was going on between you and me. So I didn't tie it up. Selfish. Not fair to anybody." We slept together that night. The loose end called and called. He must have known she would because the volume was off on the answering machine. I didn't think until much later that what he had done to her he could do to me.

At first nothing went the usual way. He didn't kiss me goodbye that morning and lose my number until Thursday. He called twice the next day. I don't think we slept apart five times in the next two months. When he asked me to move in with him after so short a time, I was surprised. I was more surprised when I did.

I loved that house. But the past started to weigh on me. At first, I thought that it was its slightly goofy inadvertent retro look that kept leading my mind away from the present. But after I started to dig around the vanity, I realized that the first owner wasn't the only ghost in the house.

The vanity was one of those things you see at Home Depot for about a hundred bucks. It didn't have drawers or rotating lazy susans or any of the other luxuries; it was just a big white box with a sink on top and a door in the front which, when opened, revealed some plumbing and a lot of stuff that probably shouldn't have been there. I decided to clean it out. I felt like an archaeologist digging through layers of ancient civilizations.

He came home when I was just finishing up. 'What are you doing?'

'Cleaning.'

'Uh. . . . I thought the place was pretty clean.'

'Well, I just opened the hallway closet and found your ex-wife in there crocheting.

So I thought it was time to get rid of some souvenirs.' I went back to my knees and continued to root through the vanity. 'You sure go through a lot of saline solution for a guy who doesn't wear contacts.' Thunk into the garbage. 'Hey, do you keep all your old toothbrushes? Good idea. Maybe you can recycle. But not now.' Thunk, thunk. 'Oh, hey, *tampons*. I know. They're for first aid. Plug bullet wounds. Quite a variety, too. Great. One for every caliber.' Thunk, thunk, thunk, *thunk*.

He found his voice. 'Ah, well, you know, you never know. . . .'

'Slut.' He looked so relieved to see me laughing.

The depression settled in just after that. At first, I wondered about the timing. It didn't make a lot of sense after all the garbage I'd been through to give in to despair when things looked good for the first time in my life. Only much later did I understand that it was the first time I'd felt safe enough to let it happen. At least down deep. On the surface I sure didn't feel anything like security. I expected him to throw me out. Instead he took care of me. He made sure that I made it to work in the morning, that I ate, that I kept my appointments with my doctors. He had always been attentive before, but I half-suspected that that was just part of the seduction; now he woke up with me in the middle of the night whenever I got scared and talked me through it until I could sleep again. I couldn't figure it out. I had never known a straight man capable of that much kindness; I thought that for a man to be that female he had to want other men.

That was my problem. Because he was different, I thought he was perfect. I should have known that he had to have the same dark side as all the others, but that he had it hidden under deeper and smoother layers of polish.

When the pictures showed up at the house, I realized my mistake. Maybe it was lucky that it happened when I was getting better. I don't know what I would have done if I was still really bad. He denied that there was anyone else. I tried to believe him. I always do; I don't know why I'm still so eager to trust the really bad ones. After the third set arrived, I knew I couldn't deceive myself any more. I started to root around for evidence of betrayal like a raccoon in a dumpster. Finally, I found a box of old photographs and letters in a dresser drawer under a stack of silk boxers. Love letters, some with perfume still clinging to them. Pictures of women, all young. All pretty. I imagined him with them, performing like an acrobat. I put them back and never told him what I found. I still tried to listen to the reassurances. The cartoons kept arriving. He kept telling me they were nothing. Nothing was one of the girls in the underwear drawer.

Whenever he kissed me, I wondered who I was tasting. Soon I wouldn't let him touch me at all. I told him I was feeling sick again. He said he understood but when he got into the shower with me in the morning and I turned away and covered my breasts he looked as though he'd been slapped. When the frustrated horny marching around got to be too much I would jerk him off, in the dark, eyes closed, counting the seconds until it was over so I could curl around the sick certainty that it was all happening again.

Him

She must have found them when I was at the gym. The house was dark when I arrived. I dropped my gym bag. "Honey, I'm home." Just like Mr. Cleaver. Pretty quiet.

They were in the kitchen. It looked like a collage. About fifteen of the cartoons had been taped to an otherwise bare wall. To each Screaming Man was attached an item of memorabilia I had thought safe in an underwear drawer. She had been busy. It must have taken her hours to arrange them. On closer inspection I saw that she hadn't stopped at simple found art. Each letter had been annotated with marginalia. Not flattering. Each photograph had gained a little word balloon containing the kind of invitation you see in ads for phone sex. I turned out the light and left the house.

Rachel

I thought that something was up when he asked to meet me someplace other than Mory's. Just coffee in the middle of the afternoon. And I knew something was up the moment he walked in. It was the first time he'd ever seemed his age. The Airedale strut was gone. He looked as though he'd had trouble shaving every morning that week. When he kissed my cheek I smelled the Camels he'd given up five years before.

"You look like hell," I said.

"Thanks, kid. That should get me through the rest of the

day." He settled back in his chair and rubbed his eyes. "Look. Bad news. Maggie left. I can't find her.'"

"Is that bad news?"

"God dammit, yes it is bad news." He caught himself. "I'm sorry. I know you didn't like her. I don't know exactly why. I just realized this, but I never told you I love her, did I? How funny. I always told you everything else. So anyway. I try to tell myself it's for the best. If she'd lose it over something like this, how could I—ah, never mind."

"Why? What was it?"

"Those fucking cartoons. I mean, they started it. You know, like a backfire starts the avalanche. At least that's what I keep telling myself. All that fucking snow was there anyway, and it would have come sliding down on me some time. As I say, I guess I'm better off that it happened now." He shook his head. His eyes looked like wet stones.

"Jesus. I really let myself hope. God damn it." The last words were meant literally and precisely. Like an objection. It was the first time I'd ever seen genuine emotion from him. It made me a little afraid.

We sat in silence. He twisted lemon into his espresso but didn't drink. Absently he stuck an end of the rind in his mouth and chewed. Finally, I couldn't stand it. "She didn't leave a note or something?"

His laugh sounded as though it hurt his throat. "Not exactly."

I didn't want to ask what that meant. "Are you still getting the cartoons?"

"Haven't for a couple of days. But there were little breaks before."

"Maybe she was sending them."

"Maybe. Maybe it was all some big crazy game to give herself an excuse to run. I doubt it. But who the hell knows."

"I still think it was Sarah."

"Yeah, well, you may be right. When she finds out about this, I'm sure she'll be satisfied." He shook his head again. "Listen, kid, I've got to go. I just wanted to tell you."

Then he was gone.

He wasn't going to get any more cartoons. I wasn't going to have any more lunches. I looked in my open purse. The original cartoon was still there. I was going to give it to him. I was going to explain it was all a joke. But it was better that he didn't know. He never would. I wonder why I thought he was so smart. Or why he thought he was so smart. I wonder what he thought was happening at all those lunches, once a week, when I kept showing up at a restaurant I didn't like, always on time, always ready to listen to whatever story he wanted to tell. I wonder if he knew what listening to those stories felt like. About the other women in his life.

He was always running out on someone. Just like my father. But this little bastard didn't get away with it.

LIKE LEONARDO'S NOTEBOOKS

He knows the phone has rung at least twice. Each time he has rolled over and seen the light struggling through the chinks in the oak Venetian blinds and moaned and rolled over again. Not to sleep; he feels too badly for that. He hasn't hurt like this since he was an undergraduate. Instead he lapses into a sweaty half-coma in which he explores his fragmentary memories of the night before like a boxer tonguing his mouth for broken teeth. The bar; wanting to leave; deciding not to; the pen; spilling breasts. Then nothing much except an indistinct impression of guiding his key into the lock in the half light of a humid August dawn.

The phone is ringing again. He rolls over in sodden, tangled 800-count sheets. The sun has overwhelmed the blinds; the bedroom is almost bright. Over the roar of the window air conditioner he can hear his neighbors at their Sunday work, car doors slamming, the creak of baby carriages, gardeners' chatter. For a long time, he wonders how this can be. Then he sees from a fluttering blind that while he was sober enough to turn on the air conditioner, he was too drunk to remember to close the windows.

Oh God, he thinks, rolling onto his back and hiding his eyes under his forearm.

Wait. What the hell was this? In blurry blue, as though written in felt tip on his sweaty skin: CAN I SEE THEM?

Oh, God. He pulls a pillow over his face and wraps his arms around it and squeezes it tight against his screwed shut eyes but it all comes back anyway.

When he got home yesterday, he thought it'd been a pretty good day.

His wife was babysitting in Westport all weekend. Trying to look like a good uncle and better husband, he went down for the day. Knowing his limits, he took his bike with him so he could abandon ship the second the Spongebob videos rolled.

So, he hammered out fifty hard miles over rolling Fairfield County hills. As he left Westport, he forgot the things that made him make the tires spin: what he would see in the office mail Monday, the way the top of his Lycra shorts rolled over love handles that weren't there a few years before. Soaked through with sweat by the time he got to Ridgefield, twenty miles from Westport, he dismounted and clacked down the street in his cleated shoes, helmet tucked under his arm. Staring at the bouncing breasts of blonde nymphets, perplexed by their failure to return his interest until he noticed his own chest jiggle in a plate glass reflection. *Oh well*, he thought, *I'm trying, anyway.*

He put the hammer down on the way back. Unobserved, he was a twelve-year-old on a Schwinn, playing fighter pilot, *vroom-vroom*ing downhill. Singing the "Battle Hymn of the Republic" as he powered up hills that he was sure would have felled a lesser man. One of whom he saw, puffing and pushing his bike uphill. He grinned and gave the fallen rider a comradely thumbs up. *Pussy*, he sneered under his breath.

But then he was home, where there was more food that he wanted but less beer than he needed. But still plenty. Happily, he forgot the Lycra waist sliding down his hips and instead thought the miles he rode as equivalent to the marathons he used to run, before the orthotics, before the torn meniscus, before the gray on his head went south to his chest. He attended to his email, each paragraph consuming a bottle.

Soon there was no more. All he had eaten that day was a muffin and a bagel; he wanted more carbs. He was starving. But rather than eat the food in the refrigerator he decided he needed just one more pint and so thinking, well, the wife is out of town, why not, he headed off to the music bar a few blocks away that he hadn't seen since he'd gotten married.

He thought the whole way that he should just eat dinner and go to bed early. But there were girls at the door of the music bar, good-looking young girls without bras, so he went in. Though it cost him three dollars to see a band he'd never heard of, he thought the money well spent because he might see more of the same girls inside. Nothing wrong with looking.

It was a long room with a bar at one side and tables at another, bisected by a shoulder-high half wall on which patrons on either side could rest their drinks. The bandstand was at the front near the windows; the walls were decorated with framed pictures of groups that hadn't performed since 1981 and mug shots of rock stars who had been arrested in this college town when the Panthers were still something to be reckoned with. At the bar itself were twenty people, equally divided between the genders, in black tee shirts or tank tops, their arms crawling with spiderwebs, crucifixes, tombstones, motorcycles. He was wearing a LaCoste polo shirt, J. Crew shorts, Kenneth Cole sandals.

He ordered a Bass and took it nervously to the shelf dividing the room. He drank the first half in two minutes. Behind him and to his left at the bar was a man arguing with a woman. He hunched into his beer and tried not to hear it. Usually if he saw a man hit a woman, he would stop it, but tonight, and in this place, perhaps he wouldn't, and if he didn't, he would rather not know he could have.

A waitress reached over him to hand a drink to a man with a shaved head and spiderwebs tattooed all over his shoulders and up to the base of his skull. Leaning over the rail to take the drink the tattooed man politely said "Excuse me."

Somehow moved by this display of courtesy, he decided that it was a good reason to get another beer. But he still knew that he was the only man in the bar in a polo shirt. So when he was halfway through this Bass and saw a stein on the bar with pens for the waitresses. He reached over and took out a blue felt tip and uncapped it and traced out a big blue diamond on the back of either hand.

He finished the beer and got another. The diamonds on his hands looked somehow empty so in one he inked, YES, the right, and NO, the left.

There was a woman nearby watching him. She sat on the last stool, the one closest to the wall. There was an empty stool between them. She was not pretty, particularly, nor was she all that young, though she was a good deal younger than he. She was wearing a black tank top and her large breasts hung over a roll of fat at the top of her jeans. Her arms were covered with blue ink that unlike his was driven below the epidermis.

"What are you doing," she asked.

"Trying to fit in," he said.

"Why?"

"Force of habit," he said, draining his glass and raising it for a refill.

"My tats tell a story."

He raised his freshened glass to his lips. "Ah," he said. "A story."

"Yes," she said. "Really."

He thought very seriously about leaving his half-finished pint on the bar and going home and going to sleep and going to Westport the next morning. But there was a band setting up and soon it would be too loud to talk, And her breasts were very large. And even though he knew that the odds against his slipping her tank top off her shoulder and lifting one up for him to suckle were vanishingly remote, the possibility that it might have would carry him through a long middle-aged night.

"So, tell me a story," he said, pouring the last of his pint down.

"Tell me yours first."

"I have no stories to tell."

"Maybe yes," she said, delicately dotting the diamond on his right hand with her index finger, and then snaking it around to his left, the one holding the pint, and tapping it as well. "And maybe no."

They both laughed. As they did, he wondered first whether she enjoyed watching him as much as he enjoyed watching her; then, ashamed, whether he shook as much as she when he laughed. But then he decided it didn't matter.

So he said, "Okay, I'll tell you a story," and he took the felt tip and wrote over the YES diamond on his right hand, crudely, because he was right handed, YOU ARE BEAUTIFUL, and as she giggled and shook her head no no, with his good right hand he wrote over the NO diamond, YES YOU ARE.

Their next beers arrived. The pile of cash in front of him wasn't enough so he added another twenty to the beer-soaked singles.

"That can't be so," she said, leaning far over to take her pint, deliberately, so that her breasts swung forward like cathedral bells.

She lifted her pint and looked up. He knew she saw him looking down. Before he could look away, she glanced at her cleavage and met his eyes. "I thank God every day," she said.

Astonished he laughed and they clinked glasses and he drained half his. He wrote on his left forearm, YOU HAVE GREAT BOOBS. She took the pen and wrote in tiny precise script, "Thanks."

Their beers gone he said, "Do you like Irish whiskey?" She nodded and he threw down another twenty and they both had doubles. Their glasses clinked again and he decided that because it was a hot night, they needed chasers so he asked the bartender for a couple of pints of Harp.

He passed her hers with his left hand and as he did he saw the gold glint on his finger and thought *well, should I slip that in my pocket,* the first time he had ever thought such a thing. And as the guilt charged down from his brain and into his curdling stomach he thought, *no need, no need, no reason to feel bad, I'm just playing.* And he realized that hand had been in front of her for an hour and it seemed to make no difference so *whew, we both know we're just playing.*

He looked at his arm where she wrote thanks. He looked at her shoulder where the strap of her tank top should be but wasn't, because it was halfway down her arm, exposing the fat full uppermost swell of a tan-lined tit. He looked over his shoulder, hoping that the bar was empty.

It wasn't. The bad news was that it was closing-time-Saturday-night-full. The good news was that it was full of Saturday night college radio nearly forty punk rock types, all pretty much hopelessly drunk and all trying to slip hands or tongues somewhere, so he didn't feel too bad about doing what he did next.

Right under where she wrote thanks he wrote, CAN I SEE THEM? He held up his arm just to make sure she could read it.

She laughed and drained her whiskey and reached over to his and drank half of what he had left. Then she pulled down his arm and held it flat against the bar and under his question wrote in big but still girlish letters, SURE.

He now sat on the next to last stool. She sat on the last. Her back was to the wall as she turned to face him. She grinned and jerked her head at the wall. He stared at her stupidly. She slipped her hands under her breasts and bounced them and jerked her head at the wall yet again.

He stumbled off his stool and, grinning, kissed her on the cheek. He planted himself with his back against the wall. "Let's see," he whispered.

She turned a hundred and eighty degrees. Her back to the barroom. "Get a load of these," she said. She slipped her tank top straps off her shoulders and shrugged and reached inside and lifted.

They dropped like hanged men. Blue-veined and stretch-marked, ragged unequal nipples reacting unequally to their sudden exposure. For just one instant he wondered what he was thinking about, but that instant passed as he took pen in hand and imagined circling each stiffening peak with sunbursts or Peter Max daisies, swooping and swirling petals in colors he didn't even have. "Oh yes," he said, casting a guilty glance at the inexplicably oblivious barroom as he lifted a half-filled water balloon.

"So beautiful," he said.

"Your John Hancock," she said.

"What?"

"I want your autograph," she said, her laughter quaking in his supporting hand. As he leaned forward to write he stumbled a little bit and caught himself on the bar with his free hand. Wondering whether it wouldn't have been better to fall forward and bury his face in the fleshy pillows. He wrote anyway. Just as he finished, he realized that perhaps he should have used a name other than his own, but he pushed that out of his mind as unworthy of a man like himself, and defiant lifted her other breast and inscribed a phone number.

"I guess I won't lose your number," she said.

"I guess not," he said.

He was still standing with his back pressed against the wall. She drained what was left in her pint of Harp. She hitched her barstool forward so that she was barely a foot away. She leaned forward. Her head was level with his navel. Her body shielded him from the bar. The bartender was busy with last call.

"My turn," she said. "My autograph."

He began to lift his shirt.

"No, no. Someplace else."

She was looking at the fly of his J Crew shorts. He stammered and pretended not to understand.

"Unless he's just big enough for my initials."

Well, hell, he thought. He handed her the pen and unzipped.

It comes back, no matter how hard he tries to hold it at bay. He lies rigid, staring at his own felt-tip handwriting. In the next room the phone rings again and he says "no, no, it didn't happen, let me just stay here until tomorrow," but when he hears a familiar voice on the answering machine he groans and throws back the sheets and stumbles into the study to hear his wife's message.

His head swimming, he stands over the phone. He has to brace himself at the desk. Without his glasses all he can see is that his arms are twined blue, like Popeye the Sailor Man's.

"Hey sleepyhead," says his wife. Her voice is so chirpy that he almost gags with shame. "I guess you're not coming down to Westport. Big night for you, Lance Armstrong. That's okay. I'm leaving now. Everybody here is okay, your nephews miss you. Hey, somebody called here this morning looking for you."

Click.

Oh God. The last broken tooth explodes in his mouth: though he used his real name, it wasn't his real number. His in-laws' was apparently the best he could think of.

He drops his head and groans. *Okay, okay,* he says to himself, *I can talk my way out of the call. I won't call back, she'll get the message, she must be used to that. But I only have forty minutes.*

So he staggers back to the bedroom and gets his glasses and looks at himself and freezes for a full minute. Then he runs downstairs and gets a can of Comet from under the sink. He gets under the shower before the water is warm and with a scrunge abrades away the evidence. Even though the water swirling down the drain is pink tinged with seeping blood, his barroom tattoos do not completely fade; after twenty minutes, his forearms and hands are still faintly blueish. Confident that his recently invented fable about an allergic reaction to Fairfield County flora will explain it all away, he is about to towel off when he realizes that he hasn't examined everything.

With less than ten minutes to go he stands dripping in the bathroom and pulls at his penis. Shriveled with hangover and shameful blue it seems to crawl into his abdomen. Where it rested safe before he left the womb. Without the slightest erotic intent, he pumps out hand cream and slathers and tugs, desperate.

Oh God. Half-hard is the best he can do, but it's enough. DEBBIE on the shaft. Well, what a lucky break, that's his wife's name, he can always say that he got really drunk and wrote her name on his dick for a joke. A possessive. See, I'm all yours.

But what about the smiley face? For a moment he wonders whether he can pass it off the same way, but even with the best faith in the world, his wife won't believe he sat in a mirror and decorated his cockhead with a sideways goatee and two staring eyes.

So he is in the shower scrubbing so hard that his tears are mixing with the spray when the bathroom door opens.

"Hello," he says, hoping that when he next tries to pee he won't find that the Comet has inflamed his urethra shut.

There is silence on the other side of the frosted glass shower door.

"I'd like some answers," she says at last.

He rolls back the door and gets out, grabbing a towel from the rack. "Hey, honey, for what?" He says, abrading himself further. "How was Westport, jeez, look at this, it's like poison ivy only worse."

"Just look at this," she says.

He glances at his battered cock free from indicting graffiti. Full of confidence he says, "Huh?"

He follows her into the bedroom. She walks the way she always walks when he has done something wrong: arms swinging at her sides, fists clenched. Sure, that he has concealed his felonies, he is prepared to admit any misdemeanor. "Did I leave the garage door unlocked again? Forget to put the milk back in the refrigerator?"

Bedroom door thrown open. She stands at the foot of the bed. "Explain this," she says.

Sheets still damp with drunken sweat have been thrown back. Their cream-colored satin stripes defaced with blurry blue.

"Look hard," she says.

Her lips are nearly white as she snaps the top sheet like a sail and lays it out over the foot of the bed.

He has had no coffee and is still stupefied with last night's beer. He thinks that he should say, "Oh God, what is it now?", but something tells him better not.

The sheets are covered with blurry blue letters, backwards, like Leonardo's notebooks. The vast mirror-texted tomes in obscure Madrid libraries and British ducal manors, describing helicopters and tanks and parachutes. But instead of marsh-draining schemes and monumental horses his Leicester Codex says WANNA FUCK and NICE NIPPLES in blurry backward scrawl. Transcribed from his own sweaty solitary flesh overnight as he tossed and mumbled like a dreaming dog suckling in its sleep.

"I can explain," he says.

"You can't," she says.

He knows she's right. But the same instinct that makes the gerbil claw and clutch at soil as it disappears down the python now drives his frantic search for an excuse. Some horrible mix-up at the laundry? Dyslexic vandals?

His heart sinks. There is no explaining this away. The python's throat has closed behind him; all that lies ahead is darkness. He sits on the edge of the bed and buries his face in his hands. "I don't know what to say," he begins. His treacherous sweat rolls down his flanks.

"You never do," she says.

"I was really drunk," he begins again, and just before confessional momentum carries him over the cliff something clicks and he screeches to a teetering halt

You never do? He's never admitted infidelity before. "I was really drunk," he says again, staring at the antique Kilim rug on the bedroom floor. His voice quivers. Slowly he realizes that it hasn't occurred to her that the hieroglyphs defacing her bedding are the product of guilty intent.

"Really," she says. "How unlike you. We'll talk about that later. But first, how the fuck did you do this? What were you doing with a Magic Marker in bed? Oh, Jesus, never mind."

Snorting with anger and disgust she began to strip the sheets from the bed. "Oh, Christ, they stink! What did you do, roll around with whores all night?"

His heart rattles his ribcage until he realizes she's kidding. She thrusts the sodden bundle into his arms.

"Throw these out. Now. That isn't coming out."

"It sure isn't," he said.

COAL TOWN HEART

Where I come from is not America at all.

Uniontown is the last province of the Hapsburg empire, a polyglot satrapy of Hungarians, Poles, Croats, Slovenians, Slovakians, Serbs, whose parents and grandparents fled the Double Eagle and instead indentured themselves to the Consolidation Coal Company. As you come into town on Route 51, from Pittsburgh, where the coal went, you see at Five Corners the bronze effigy of a doughboy, his bayoneted rifle held negligently in one hand, the other on his hip, his tin hat tilted rakishly as a gangster's fedora, standing guard before the universal small-town tablet of war dead.

In his place should be Franz Josef, sceptered and sabred, side-whiskers trailing onto Imperial ermine. His Imperial chin, happily free of the family curse, arrogantly thrust at passing motorists who but for the grace of God would have fed his dynasty's draft.

Were Franz Josef to stand where he should, his basilisk stare would meet a senior housing project. The tallest building in town, eleven proud stories of glazed brick, centrally air conditioned, monument to an effusion of Federal money in the 1970's. Franz would grind his bronze teeth in Holy Roman rage, not because he spent half the day in its proletarian shadow, but because of what it replaced.

The senior project was built when I was already old enough to shave. It rose on the rubble of what I had always thought of as the Addams Family mansion, a boarded-up Victorian pile of cupolas and scrimshaw, stucco walls long since bleached palest yellow, mortar decalcifying under the patient parasitism of strangling ivy. But I was told that it was no such thing; rather, it was the home of the Princess of Taxes, a European aristocrat who had spent her last days in Uniontown, PA.

I never believed in the Princess. Though my aunts may have believed in their girlhood that FDR had an office in the Fayette Bank Building and received Churchill at the Hotel Summit, I cannot recall a time when I thought the world so small and Uniontown so great that I would have believed that anyone of consequence would have taken ship from Hamburg to dock on the shores of the Redstone Creek. And later, I rolled an adolescent eye at the obviously mythic title: Princess of Taxes? Right; widow of the tax collector of Fayette County.

But every man over a certain age had memories of the Princess he was eager to share. All variations on a theme: A limousine, vast but ancient, its tire shredded as it listed in a ditch, in its saloon a desiccated beauty wrapped in furs, chewing her ivory cigarette holder and waving a champagne flute in frustration as her shaven-headed chauffeur tried to flag down a 1940's American boy who knew how to use a tire iron and could thus be rewarded with a ducat.

Right, I thought: In the back, Gloria Swanson; at the wheel, Erich von Stroheim; but you, my friend, are no William Holden. Nice try, though. Nice to make a Princess out of a rich old crazy woman in a big old house.

But it was true. At least, that there had been a Princess in Uniontown. Perhaps even now her ghost rides the elevators in the senior center, and on Wednesday afternoons furiously rearranges bingo markers when their owners aren't looking.

For in 1911, Lida Eleanor Nicholls of Brownsville, Pa, married Prince Viktor von Thurn und Taxis, scion of a family descended from the hereditary Postmaster General of the Holy Roman Empire, in Uniontown. After the Prince had breathed his last in Vienna in 1928, true to her coal-town heart, she came back to Uniontown to die.

She married him at the best time, the time just before his world was swept away, when she could as a new bride run laughing down the halls of a schloss in East Prussia counting the antlers of slain chamois hovering between leatherbound books and coffined ceiling, and pirouette, still laughing, and collapse in a heap when her count reached five hundred.

This Brownsville girl who still a young wife would travel with her husband in a private railway car to Vienna. Where she would make her best curtsey to an old man who would extend to her a hand that had shaken Metternich's, a hand that had touched a hand that had touched Napoleon's, and lift her up and present her to his son, a man himself already a grandfather and who in a few years would drive through Sarajevo in an open car like JFK and like JFK die in a hail of inexplicable bullets. Whose death would send millions to their ends in equally inexplicable rains of lead.

Talleyrand—friend of Metternich whose hand shook the hand of the Austrian Emperor whose hand she touched—said that no one who had not known the world before the French Revolution could know the sweetness of life. But our Brownsville girl knew another sweet world, a world before the

Second Somme and the trenches squelching with the clotted blood of their fallen defenders. After she kissed the Emperor's hand in Vienna, she traveled east to St Petersburg to curtsey before the Czar; later she would go west to bow her head before a little man with a withered arm in Berlin. And she went further west, to Britain, to shooting parties at Sandringham, where the King-Emperor, lord of a quarter of the earth's land surface and all of its seas, devoted his weekends to blowing grouse in their hundreds from a lowering English sky.

And in all this time the girl from Brownsville kept up her bargain with the Prince. That for every time she dropped in royal curtsey to a crowned head she dropped in carnal curtsey to her husband. Her husband, heir to a name that had once been one with the Imperial Post Office, winced in shame as *margrafen,* whose most distant ancestors bent under the Order of the Golden Fleece, smirked and tittered as he marched his wife down a double row of jackbooted dragoons, sabers drawn, to be presented to a little man with a big moustache and that withered arm. A husband who wondered as the Kaiser lifted his wife to her feet with his one good arm whether His Imperial Majesty had heard the stories that made the *margrafen* giggle. Whether the Kaiser wondered if the Princess who knelt before him would unbutton his fly and reach into his breeches as she had for so many men before her present husband.

A present husband who knew his wife for what she was before he married her and so took the Brownsville girl back down Unter den Linden in his growling Lagonda to a Baroque townhouse and arranged her on a red satin sofa, naked, in a room hung with tapestries of the Bavarian hunt, where she played with herself to the polite applause of monocled Junkers with foot-long ivory cigarette holders and bored wives who had seen the same more times than they cared to remember. A husband who sat in the last row of gilt Rococo chairs and embarrassed his guests with the wildness of his applause at his wife's public climax.

A Brownsville wife who nevertheless smiled and clung to her husband's arm as the photographers detonated their flash powder while they strolled down Cunard gangplanks into ports wide open before August 1914. Who loyally clung to her husband's friends when his world was split asunder as the trenches bisected Belgium. Writing them thank you's for the hampers from Fortnum's and notes of condolence when their lordling sons fell flaming from the skies or coughed up their lives in the thick yellow haze of mustard gas with which the Junkers smothered their trenches. As those brave Oxonian lieutenants tried to keep up the Tommies' spirits with music hall songs from the days before the war.

A Brownsville princess who when the war was nearing its end tried to forget that the bandages she rolled with her few remaining maids would plug wounds inflicted by her own countrymen. Terrified boys from Montana and New York and perhaps even Brownsville, thrown into the Argonne Wood when the French had mutinied and the English simply had no more to give, to drive her husband the Prince's people back past their last lines of defense. What did she think as she wiped the fever sweat from the brow of a dying Pomeranian Grenadier in the hospital at which she volunteered? Perhaps when her husband, grand in a staff colonel's uniform, came home after midnight laughing with news of London zeppelin raids and Russia's collapse, she pleasured him into a stupor and then wept herself to sleep, biting her knuckles as she thought of the Sargent Yorks disintegrating under big Hunnish artillery shells. Perhaps when her husband came home early, in November 1918, and slumped in his chair and said, *we are lost,* she kissed his pomaded head and filled his glass again and again until it finally fell from his fingers and crashed into a thousand crystal fragments on marquetry floor. To sing, just audibly, just to herself, after she had closed the big double doors on her snoring Prince, as she swept down the gilded hallway to her own room, *I'm A Yankee Doodle Dandy.*

But perhaps not. She stayed with her Prince when the bad days came. When the men who had been foolish enough to destroy her borrowed world deemed themselves wise enough to make a new one. When the Kaiser was gone and the Czar dead. As her husband's Germany submerged under tides of street armies proclaiming Marxist soviets or Hohenzollern restorations, she and the Prince scuttled to the relative quiet of Vienna barely in time to see the last Hapsburg, Carl—Franz Josef not having lived to see his patrimony ripped asunder in Versailles—himself scuttle away with barely a dozen hussars to remind him of what he had been cheated.

Leaving our Brownsville aristocrat to recreate herself as a Jazz Princess. Her husband's money evaporating in Weimar inflation, his Berlin Baroque townhouse now a Vienna Beidermeir apartment, string quartets and waltzes now a gramophone and Charlestons.

Somehow, in Vienna, she for the first time shone in her own right. In this necropolis between East and West, capital of an ossified empire whose final collapse had taken down with it an entire world. Not so long ago, before the old world dissolved in the trenches, her transatlantic origins barred her from the choicest Berlin salons. No longer; as estates granted by Charlemagne were confiscated by Slovenian nationalists or foreclosed by Dutch bankers, it was her name, rather than the prince's, that appeared on guest lists. Americanness and title suddenly intersected to open every door.

Her limousine, escutcheoned with sixteen quarterings of nobility, pulled up to basement rathskellers from which American jazz wailed. In those smoky caverns, she took as lovers French musicians or bankrupt counts.

In these pursuits her husband was an only occasional obstacle. His brain bowed under the weight of defeat, syphilis, and gin, he generally made his presence felt only on predawn rambles through the apartment after which she explained his howlings to neighbors as the result of a head wound in the Great War. On evenings increasingly rare, he arranged his little tableaux, just like the old days, with audiences smaller and shabbier on each performance, to which she readily agreed, certain that her compliance secured his complaisance.

One such evening, however, the audience was singular. In the salon hung with hunting tapestries, the Prince was alone. He sat in a chair whose gilded arms were twisted in the shapes of dolphins and tritons, whose needlepoint back was worked with his family's arms at Gobelins when Louis XV was still a bachelor. His wife reclines naked in a red satin chaise lounge, just like the old days, waiting irritably for what would come next.

The tapestries thrust away. From either side cavalrymen, two from the left, one from the right, young, obviously drunk, swagger in. She ignores the reek of garlic and beer and expertly unbuttons their flies. Within a minute their breeches have fallen around their boots and the Prince is shrieking encouragement. Hands and mouth occupied she steals a glance at the Louis XV throne, where the Prince flails away at his stubbornly flaccid cock.

The boys are finished soon. The Prince has been silent a while. She sits up, disturbing the viscous puddle that has formed on her belly.

Again? Says the boldest of the hussars. His friends laugh and wink.

Get out, she says. Now.

We were just getting started, says the hero.

Get out or I'll call the police.

The hero laughs and strokes himself. He was still a boy when the war began, but he remembers his father and grandfather and uncles crawling to women like this, tugging forelocks, knuckling foreheads, grinning and scraping in stables and sculleries. He will tell the Princess what he thinks of women like her.

Before the hero can reply he glances at his audience. The Prince sprawls sideways in his Louis XV throne, eyes rolled back behind lids at half-mast. A puddle of urine on the marquetry floor between his feet. His tongue, purple and bleeding, caught between his teeth. One outthrust arm twitching, its fingers clicking as though playing a castanet, the other modestly cupping his genitals.

As the bravest hussar watches, the Prince struggles for breath. Once. Twice. His tongue still caught between his teeth. Snoring like a basset hound. Suddenly still.

The Princess is staring at her husband. Her face expressionless. For a while there is silence. Fabric rustles; she looks up. The boys have disappeared behind the tapestries.

The Prince's brother arrives at breakfast. Murmurous undertakers, schooled in the hatchments and black plumes attending the funeral of an heir to the Imperial Post Office, have already laid out the Prince in his bedroom. His hands decorously folded over a red scarlet coverlet worked with the double eagle in gilt thread. As the princess shares coffee with her brother-in-law, the undertakers discreetly measure stairs and hallways for their capacity for a coffin.

The Prince's brother—himself also a Prince under the Imperial constitution; without duels and cavalry charges and suicide, Europe would long since have collapsed under the accumulated weight of its Highnesses—is magnificent in black cutaway and striped trousers. His mustache is artfully groomed to conceal a harelip. His grief is even less visible.

He sips coffee and dabs linen at his deformity. Don't worry, he says, you will be taken care of. And I'm sure you agree that there will be no need to discuss these sad circumstances.

Of course, she says, avoiding the implication that she needed taking care of. He had a stroke. You know that there are others?

The brother-in-law nods. He winks, surprisingly jovial given the occasion. I know their colonel.

His cup is empty. He stands. My sisters will call this afternoon. He kisses her hand.

Her sisters-in-law arrive in dressed in mourning from different centuries. The younger has adopted what her mother must have worn for the funeral of Empress Elizabeth forty years ago: black taffeta and lace and a ribboned bonnet. Her older sister is up to date in ebony sheath and cloche hat that does little to flatter a lower jaw that protrudes so far that it looks as though her servants must chew her food for her. Like their brother, they have concealed their grief perfectly; unlike their brother, they no longer see a reason to treat her as anything other than a whore.

You will be leaving Vienna, says the younger. Her tone is equidistant between question and command. Prim mouth and bulging eyes; she looks like a squirrel.

I may, says the Princess.

Our lawyers will call on you, says the older, speaking slowly. The jaw that advertises her genuine Imperial connection makes it difficult for her to articulate.

I will be happy to receive them, says the Princess. With barely the conventional expressions of condolence, the sisters are gone.

That evening the Princess is busy. She lets it be known that her house will be open to her friends, even in mourning. She takes counsel from the morganatic widows and bankrupt counts who detour to her apartments on their way to the cabarets. They urge her to get her own lawyer, one whom they describe with fingers raised to their own noses in Semitic hooks and in accents of lisping Yiddish caricature. Almost always using the same name, and always the same tribe.

The next afternoon the Princess takes a closed car, without coat of arms, curtains drawn across saloon windows, to a side street off the Ringstrasse, not far from the Spanish Riding School. A street broad by the standards of the eighteenth century, its cobblestones making the tires stutter; on either side creamy stucco facades broken at regular and frequent intervals by big casement windows. At Maria Theresa street; a street down which Voltaire may have walked on his route from France to Prussia and Frederick the Great.

Before the car has even stopped a porter darts from the doorway to which she is bound. White tie and black cutaway, massive English umbrella overpowering a Vienna mist. He opens the door and bows her forward. He opens another door, folds his umbrella with a murmured apology, and decorously follows her up the single carpeted flight to the office.

It is not what she expects. She thought that a Hungarian Jew whose banker father had bought a barony before the war would surround himself in legitimizing mahogany and leather and brass. That he himself would be fat, pince-nezed, bearded, his extra chins thrust upward from a starched wing collar cinched tight with an Ascot tie.

But the office into which she is led is as bright and open as these precincts will allow, the desk a piece of blonde wood that could disappear in the fittings of an ocean liner's lounge, white walls hung with unframed oils streaked with ragged colors. Behind the desk a slender young man in dove gray flannel rises to greet her.

Princess, he says, accept my condolences for your loss. He bows her to a chair, black leather slings stretched between chrome tubes. As soon as her mourning veil is lifted, he offers a Virginia cigarette and fire from a Ronson.

He lights one himself and settles behind his ocean liner desk. Please, he says.

I think my late husband's family may make difficulties, she says.

They will, he says.

I think my late husband had financial difficulties, she says.

He did, he says. Forgive me, but I have made inquiries.

They sit in silence for a moment, enjoying their cigarettes.

So, she says. She abandons her Imperial diction. She is, after all, a Brownsville Princess. How bad is it?

He taps feathery ash into a crystal tray. Not good.

She leans forward to deposit ash as well. She raises her eyebrows and waits.

The Prince was never as wealthy as he seemed, says the lawyer. He was still very rich. But nevertheless, after your marriage he borrowed money against his lands and his incomes to finance the way you lived. Had the Central Powers won the War, things would have been different. He taps ash from his cigarette again. But they did not. And they are not. The mortgaged lands have been seized in the new countries made in Versailles. His rents from the estates in Austria and Germany do not pay the interest on his debts. Speaking of rent, your apartment in the Ring is two years in arrears.

He leans forward and folds his hands on the leather blotter on his blonde wood desk. Forgive me, Princess, he says, moving his eyes from her white face to the cigarette burning dangerously close to her fingers, but there is also a child from a previous entanglement who makes claim on his estate.

A child? A *child? Him?*

I understand, Princess, that given his proclivities it was unlikely. But he was young, and he acknowledged the outcome. Thus, the estates are burdened with that as well.

She stubs out her cigarette. So there is nothing?

Very little, says the lawyer. Perhaps nothing.

So when his family says they'll take care of me, what does that mean?

Very little, says the lawyer. Perhaps nothing.

Moments pass. She can hear the clop-clop of horses and the growl of the cars that will shortly displace them. So, she says. What should I do?

Perhaps another cigarette? No? He closes the silver case on his *Normandie* desk. Well. You know I am a Jew?

Yes.

My people are often accused of avarice in matters of money. He shrugs. Perhaps at times that has been true. But I will tell you, Princess, that whatever my people have done, whatever they have been driven by necessity to do, it is nothing compared to what noble families in this city, the oldest families, the best families, have done.

He reaches forward and takes another cigarette from his transatlantic case. He settles back in his chair and squints through coiling smoke. They will fight like snakes over whatever little is left.

I thought, she says, that you have done well in court.

I have, he says. I have done very well. When two Jew lawyers fight for two princely families I will usually win. But when a Jew lawyer fights for an American wife against a princely family, I will lose. He takes a long drag from his cigarette. And there is little to fight over anyway.

The office is heavy with silence and smoke. Okay, she says, her Imperial diction slipping further, what do I do?

He stubs out the cigarette. He leans forward conspiratorially. Do you have jewels?

Yes.

Yours, those he gave you, as well as the family's?

Yes.

Are there things around the apartment of value—books, tapestries, silver—things that you could pack and move?

Yes.

Then, he says, leaning further forward, his tobacco-scented

breath in her face, tonight, pack them all, tell your servants to take a holiday because you're in mourning except one or two you trust, take everything of value and take a night train to Paris and sell it. Then take the cash and go back to America.

She is stunned. America?

America.

Tonight?

Tonight. I know, I know, your husband's funeral is tomorrow. I will tell the family that you are so undone by grief you had to leave. And I will express surprise when they visit your apartment and see it stripped bare.

Now please, Princess, he says, rising, go. He extends his hand.

She takes it. What must I pay you?

Nothing, he says.

Nothing? She says. But—

Pay a Hungarian Jew lawyer nothing? He laughs. What? Princess, please believe charity is not exclusively Christian. He bows her to the office door and bends to kiss her hand. And in any event, I imagine I will soon be doing the same myself. Have you not seen the flyers in the street? Those passed around by the young men in the brown shirts? Princess, you and I are birds of a feather. You fly a little earlier.

The closed car waits on the street. The lawyer's porter stands beside it under his big English umbrella. Bowing, he opens the door and raises the umbrella. Wait, she says as she slides in. She reaches into her bag and pulls out her notecase. She scribbles for a moment. There are three messages. She folds them neatly and writes a name and address on the back of each. Around them she wraps banknotes with many zeroes; a fortune before the war, but still a good dinner after.

These have to be delivered in the next hour. Can you? I can't go home unless you can.

If the porter sees the banknote his face doesn't show it. Please, Princess, he says, go home.

Thank you, she says.

She very much wants a drink but she knows that if she has one she will have three and if things don't work as she intends that will be very bad. She tells the chauffeur to drive to a café near St Stephens; when he gets there, she tells him she's changed her mind and wants to walk while having a cigarette and that he should meet her in front of the Sacher.

When she finally arrives more than two hours have passed since she left the lawyer's. She has had six cigarettes and three cups of coffee. Her limousine has blocked traffic for at least an hour. As the chauffeur leaps out to open her door, she endures an angry buzz in half a dozen accents from hotel guests, fat with sachertorte, whose Viennese evenings have been delayed. English, French, even her American, growling angrily, we won this war, why do we have to wait?

When they arrive at her building another doorman holds open another vast umbrella. As her chauffeur assists her out, he finds pressed in his hand banknotes wrapped around gold. The next few days will be hard, she says. Take care of those who come for my husband. Now, goodnight.

Princess, he says, bowing low.

She turns to the porter. I will need your help tonight.

You will not be disturbed, Princess, says the porter. He stares at the chauffeur as he counts his money.

That is not what I mean, she says. You will be. She is nervous; if her notes were not delivered things will be very bad.

The chauffeur slams his door and edges into the sparse traffic of a beaten city.

Princess, says the porter. Your servants are gone. I have two men upstairs with crates. Cars will be here when you need them to go wherever you need them to go.

The Brownsville girl wants to weep, to throw her arms around the porter's neck, to kiss his cheeks. But there are still couples on the street in white tie and ostrich boa; the porter's pronouns are still formal; and she is still, however briefly, the widow of an heir to the Imperial Post Office. So instead she presses into the porter's hand a metal disk weighing nearly an ounce, a circle of gold stamped with the profiles of Franz Josef and his long dead Elizabeth, a coin that could buy the porter a bad farm.

Another when we're done, she says.

This is enough, Princess, he says.

Say that then, she says.

He holds the door open and she walks up the stairs acutely aware of the lightness of her purse; if the prince's family strikes first, the porter is now worth more than she.

The apartment. Nearly silent. In the anteroom, beside a dozen big wooden crates, their roughness an insult to the marquetry panels, the two men the porter had promised. Middle-aged veterans they remember their prewar manners and pull off their caps as she enters. One says, whenever you're ready, ma'am, we have no place else to go. He has an eyepatch. His friend's lower jaw is altogether gone, and she sees in his throat just over the open collar the silver tube of a whistler, maimed by a bullet or shell fragment so that he can no longer speak, but instead warbles in a chickadee code. As she stares the whistler winks, and replacing his cap, tweets what she thinks must be a friendly greeting.

Her ladysmaid enters the room. Princess, we don't have much time.

The Princess moves fast. Her bedroom. Her maid has already spread every suitcase she owns open over her bed. In one goes the cheap paste, the everyday stuff. In another the jewels she pulls out of her dresser, nothing special, Wednesday night diamonds. Then the contents of her case, the good things, the tiara she wore when she bowed to the Kaiser and the Czar, the heavy emerald drops that hung from her ears when she played bridge with George V.

Her ladysmaid snaps up the case and says, Shall we go?

The Brownsville girl says, Not yet, let's see what the Prince had.

But Princess, says the ladysmaid, he's still there.

The Princess winks at her maid and says, He won't mind.

The Prince's coffin lies beside his bed. Elegant ebony with his arms on its lid in gilt and enamel. Lid open to receive him for tomorrow's funeral.

The Prince himself in his canopied bed. Dead two days, livid and swollen. Hands crossed across his chest discreetly bound with silk thread. Jaw wrapped shut with a bandage as though he suffered from toothache. Eyes closed with coins, mere pennies.

The Princess and her ladysmaid stand at the bedroom's open door.

I'm sorry, says the Princess, averting her eyes as the maid gags into her handkerchief. I'll open the windows. Did you remember the bag?

The Princess tears open drawers. Into the leather satchel go diamond-edged miniatures of Louis XV, Augustus the Strong, George II. The goggle-eyed kings disappearing under platinum cigarette cases chased with the arms of emperors and their affectionate remembrances to the Prince's father, uncles, cousins. Another drawer: cases of dueling pistols, the oldest percussion cap barkers made in London in 1799 for Beau Brummel, the most recent smooth-and-singles that had settled disputes of honor in the Wald just before the war. As the Princess cracks their case she smells gunpowder and wonders who won.

The bag is now almost too heavy for her to carry and the room is still fat with treasure. She inclines her head at her ladysmaid. The girl, bent double under the satchel's weight, whines into the hallway.

The Princess' lip curls with sour satisfaction at the girl's absence as she opens another drawer. Subdivided into a dozen sliding compartments. She knew the Prince would have such a hiding place.

A cigar cutter shaped like a satyr bending over a nymph, the cutting edge a sickle that jets from his loins into hers. A portrait miniature of a decorous eighteenth-century couple, the man ribboned with the order of St Louis; its jeweled edge contains a snap that reveals another portrait within, the noble naked save for his Order, his wife kneeling on a chair guiding in his impossible member. Volumes bound in calfskin, printed on vellum, their pages littered with men and women naked chained and racked.

The ladysmaid is back with more bags. The Princess blinks hard, twice, and the images of her honeymoon in the East Prussian schloss and what she had hoped for are gone. Twice more and the reality is gone too. She dumps the Prince's secret cache into a valise herself and snaps it shut.

The Prince's jewelry case: tie pins, rings, daytime cufflinks, five sets of studs. Enamel, precious and semiprecious stones, cloisonne. The ladysmaid says, now, Princess?

She sweeps from her husband's room. Behind her the whistler and the ladysmaid, who closes the bedroom door with evident relief and the Sign of the Cross. Now, she says to the whistler, big boxes, big enough to hold pictures. She looks at her watch. And tell your friend we need cars in an hour. For the station. Twice as many as you think we need for what we have now. And when you come back, bring a screwdriver.

The whistler chirps and nods. As he trots down the hall the Princess believes his eyes are merry.

The ladysmaid is crying. Highness, she says, I don't think this is right.

The Brownsville princess thinks about putting her arm around the shoulders of a poor provincial girl not so different from herself when an heir to the Imperial Post Office lifted her from the obscurity of southwestern Pennsylvania. It isn't, she will say, but I'm just a poor girl like you, what can I do, I just lost my husband, you know how these people are.

Instead she grabs the ladysmaid's shoulders and says, look at me. And when the ladysmaid does she slaps her hard, twice.

The crying stops.

Now, says the Princess. Do you stay here in Vienna and live on whatever they drop from their table or come with me to Paris or wherever I go and take your chance?

The girl raises her tear-stained face. Wherever you go, Princess.

Good.

The whistler is back with his boxes and tools. The Princess has already decided that the Meissen is too numerous and too delicate to move, and the Delft too common to bother with. But she knows the durable, the good, and the readily-converted. Thus, two Watteau oils are wrapped and carefully boxed, followed by three drawings regularly, but not reliably, attributed to Rembrandt. The hunting prints, worth less than their frames, she leaves to her sisters-in-law. But the ormolu mounts on Louis XVI consoles fall to the whistler's screwdriver, and a pair of Empire gilt-bronze sconces wind up boxed.

The ladysmaid is back. Princess, she says, the cars are outside. It's three o' clock.

The Princess is handing a pair of candelabra to the whistler. There is nothing with which to wrap them; the strips of chamois and bolts of flannel are gone.

One minute, says the Princess. She winks at the whistler. The whistler winks back. Then he turns to the ladysmaid and winks at her and chirps like a finch.

The Princess runs to the little salon with the red silk divan. A tapestry, long and narrow, hangs over the doorway to the back stairs up which her lovers trooped in their twos and threes for an evening's entertainment. No wider than a door and not much longer. Sixteenth-century Flemish, the Prince once told her, from a cartoon by Raphael, the Siege of Jerusalem by Frederick Barbarossa with my ancestor the Count of Thurn holding his stirrup.

She tugs. It stays where it is. She tugs again, harder. Fabric rips; nails pop out; it is on the floor. A square foot of silk and wool stays anchored to the wall over the backstairs doorway.

She is back in the entry. Here, she says, use this.

The man with the eye patch and the porter have been busy. Only one box is left and the tapestry soon pads its contents. She and the ladysmaid and the whistler are on the street. Vienna is at last silent and as dark as a city can ever be, in the hour before the horizon ceases to be utterly black.

There are four cars at the curb. Each sags visibly at its burdened trunk. Princess, says the porter. Should I call for more? The train is in two hours.

The Princess laughs. She doesn't know why; it seems the only thing to do. She wants to tell him, yes, more cars, let me take everything; she wants to say no, unload these things, I'm staying. I want to go home, I want to go back to where I come from, I want to be in my home town where I was poor but I want to go there rich; I want to be right here, I want to be around kings and queens and jazz musicians, but I want this to be my home town where people love me just the way I am. I want to weep at my husband's funeral but I don't want to remember what I had to do to be his wife.

Still smiling she turns to the porter. No, she says, this is enough. She fumbles in her purse for another of the big coins.

Princess, says the porter. That was enough. He clicks his heels and bows and opens the door of the first car. The Princess enters, followed by the ladysmaid. As soon as they are settled the whistler makes as if to enter too, but the ladysmaid pushes him back. He shrugs his disappointment but grinning as best as he can without a lower jaw he lifts his cap as the porter slams the door.

The Princess turns to the rear window as her convoy pulls away from the curb. The porter's white-gloved hand is raised in salute; the whistler's cap is waving in little circles. The Princess settles back against the stiff leather and determinedly stares at the back of the driver's head, sure that if she looks at what she is leaving she will throw open the door and throw herself rolling onto the Ringstrasse, crying, but I married you, I married this place, I married these things, don't make me go back.

But she does not. As the car growls to the station, to the raised eyebrows of customs agents and border guards and perhaps acquaintances perplexed by the widow's flight, her attention remains fixed on a stubborn carbuncle on the driver's neck.

Her ladysmaid breaks the silence. Are we going to Amsterdam, Princess?

At first, she says.

Paris, then? Says the ladysmaid, unable to conceal her excitement.

Next, says the Princess. She wonders how the driver's barber can shave his neck without drawing blood.

Will we stay there, Princess?

No. Then Hamburg.

Hamburg? Princess, we're staying in *Hamburg?* The ladysmaid is tired and so can be forgiven the note of hysteria.

Don't worry, says the Princess. We're not staying in Hamburg. We're taking a ship.

Ah, London? New York? Oh, wonderful, New York!

Perhaps. You'll see.

The ladysmaid sinks back. Tired as she is her face is alight with the glow of Manhattan, Buenos Aires, Lisbon. Her eyelids flutter over dreams of cocktail parties and polo matches.

The Princess allows her to snore the fifteen minutes to the station. She sees no reason to tell her where their trunks will at last be unpacked.

A FRAGMENT FROM RAYMOND CHANDLER'S FIRST SCENARIO FOR THE SOPRANOS

I was shaving my balls when the phone rang.

I dropped the Mach 3 and my scrotum. With my right hand I pulled the Lucky out of my mouth and with the left cradled the receiver. I got shaving cream on both.

"Yeah," I said.

"What're you doing?" said Jimmy the Bedwetter.

"Shaving my balls," I said. I flicked the Barbasol off the Lucky with my thumbnail and stuck it back in my mouth.

Jimmy the Bedwetter laughed. I don't like it when he laughs. It makes me want to stop smoking. "Hey, that's really funny," he said.

"It isn't funny. I was really shaving my balls."

The Bedwetter paused to consider this news. "No kidding? What the fuck for? It's fucking February, for Christ's sake."

I moved the jewels a little to the left and squinted through smoke to attack a particularly tough follicle. "February? So what if it's February?"

"It ain't hot enough to shave your balls. You don't need to

shave your balls until May. April, maybe. If you wear wool pants. Not February. Not unless you wear fur pants and I know for a fucking fact you don't."

"That I don't," I said. I thought for a minute. Maybe I shouldn't have said anything but I had to know. "So you shave your balls in the spring?"

"Fuck yes. Maybe not spring. Maybe early summer. Usually Memorial Day for sure. Why?"

The Lucky was going to burn my lips in a minute but I dragged on it hard anyway. I decided not to tell him about the crabs. I decided that maybe I wanted to kill myself before I talked to him again.

"So Jimmy," I said. I spat the smoldering butt into the ashtray so I could concentrate on my perineum. Soon as I finished there was a bottle of Old Infidelity and a chess problem that needed work.

"So what?"

"So why'd you call?"

"Hey not to talk about your fucking balls that's for sure. But hey maybe I did. Something you need to know. Fishlip Billy got whacked."

The Teflon blade poised over an artery I really didn't want to nick. "Fishlip Billy? From Justin the Rectum's crew?"

"Fuckin A."

"So what's it to me?" I knew it was something and I didn't want to finish defoliating if he was going to say something that made my hands shake.

"Just this. He had your card in his pocket. And Lloyd the Jew says the LAPD wants to talk to you about it."

I was trying to figure out what that meant. I was also trying to figure out how to get another Lucky without getting it all covered with Barbasol. "Thanks. Thanks Jimmy."

"Hey," he said. "No problem. Hey, don't your balls get cold when you shave them this early?"

"Nah," I said.

"Fuck," he said, and hung up.

I dropped my ballsack and stood up. My pants were still around my ankles so I had to take little baby steps to the window. I got shaving cream all over the blinds as I parted them to peer out. The sun had gone down half an hour before and the drunken boulevards were just coming to life.

Jimmy the Bedwetter. Fishlip Billy. Justin the Rectum. Lloyd the Jew.

It was going to be like that.

CHANGELING

When she saw what the dog had in its mouth, she screamed so hard that a vessel burst in her throat. She fainted and fell on her back. The blood poured into her lungs. She would have died on the kitchen floor. But because the mill closed early her husband came home to find her.

Three days before, her baby had taken his own desperate gasps, a dozen all he had in this life. When she stopped crying and fell asleep her husband pried the little body out of her arms and wrapped it in newspapers and twine. There were five other children, still alive, in the two rooms of their tarpaper shack past the end of a dirt road near the ridge line. FDR had yet to bring Happy Days Here Again to Osage, West Virginia. Until then there wasn't going to be money for a funeral or even spare sheets for a shroud.

He went behind the house and up to the treeline. With a summer Appalachian downpour beating on his back he scooped out a grave with a few turns of a shovel and laid his baby in it.

When he told his wife what he had done she cried harder than she thought she had tears for. She swore and swung at him. Her nails raked his cheek. Because he was ashamed, this once he took it.

For days she lay in bed and listened to the rain drum on the plywood and tarpaper above her. She thought of the baby sleeping in the mud. But at last she remembered the babies who had lived and got out of bed.

Still heavy with birth, she waddled into the kitchen. There was a little window over the big tin tub that was her sink. She braced her hands on either side of the tub and stared out the window, getting used to sunlight again. Halfway between the outhouse and the treeline she could see a dog scrabbling in the mud. It was a colorless medium-sized coonhound that someone had got tired of feeding and thrown stones at until it finally got the message.

Blinking in the rain-filtered morning light she watched the dog frantically delve. Because she liked dogs, she smiled a little as it stopped and beat its tail in triumph. When the dog planted its hind legs and pulled harder, she laughed, expecting a Walt Disney dinosaur bone to pop out of the earth to dwarf the industrious pooch.

What the dog had in its teeth was a tiny arm, bluish gray. Just as she recognized it for what it was her baby was free from the mud. Teeth in the abdomen, the dog gave it one triumphant shake and trotted off into the woods.

After her husband found her and shook her and shook her until the screaming stopped, she stayed in bed for another long time. The rain had ended. She had nothing to listen to except what was inside her head.

The first time she got up her husband came home from the mill to find her filthy with cracked and bleeding nails. She explained with the utmost patience that she had gone into the woods to find where the dog had buried its bone.

At first, he reasoned with her, and then he prayed over her, and when that didn't work, he beat her until she promised to stay close to the house. But he came home to find his yard cratered with shallow pits she had dug with their soup ladle.

He tied her to the bed that night. The next day she swore she'd be good. With five children, the youngest just a year old, he figured he didn't have much choice. So he let her loose.

Because there was a lot of work at the mill that week, it was late when he got home. Even though it was midsummer, the light had almost faded from the ridgeline as he made his way up the switchbacked trail to the house. She sat on the unpainted two-by-four steps that were their porch. He smiled because she rocked a blanketed bundle in her arms. Their youngest. He thought, she's getting better. Still smiling he leaned forward to kiss the child she held up to him.

He spent the rest of his life trying to convince himself that his lips never touched what she had wrapped in the blanket. Gagging, he struck it away. She screamed and fell on him with teeth and fists. It took the two oldest to help him tie her to the bed with belts. He sent the middle boy to get the county doctor.

When the doctor arrived, her head had been beaten in against the iron bedstead. Her husband explained that she must have done it while he was out in the yard waiting.

The doctor listened to the story. Night had fallen long ago and his car was parked at the end of the road, nearly a thousand yards away. There was blood on the husband's hands. Misadventure, said the doctor. Death by misadventure.

The husband nodded. In his hands was a baby blanket to which shreds of mangy fur and leathery dried skin still clung.

The doctor left as fast as he could. As he hurried his feet crunched scattered marsupial bones and a possum's skull wrapped in a blue bonnet.

Acknowledgements

I started my first book when I was in second grade. It began, and ended, "during world war 2." I did not capitalize the initial D. I didn't know I was supposed to.

Eight years later I launched another effort, a protracted exercise in science-fiction plagiarism called *The Peacemakers' War*. It distracted me through the dark heart of adolescence. It was typed, night after night, on an upright Royal manual. Luckily the manuscript does not survive.

It was not until I was well into my thirties that Pat Kaplan, in a transformational moment, gave me the gentle push that led, as much as any one thing, to an effort to achieve the goal I had held since childhood. I will always be grateful.

Likewise appreciated are the generous and tireless mentorship of Tom Perrotta and the late Richard Selzer. Also, without the friendship and support of stalwarts John Crowley, Trey Ellis, Lou Bayard, Julie Glass, and Shawn Crawford, surely I would have faltered.

Thanks are due as well to Charles Clifford Brooks III, the old-school poet and gentleman who brought me onto the *Blue Mountain Review*. So too Lisa Kastner, publisher and literary entrepreneur, who saw some promise in these efforts, and Peter

Wright, the editor who contributed so much to realizing it.

I hope my nieces and nephews Jared, Alec, Evan, Emily, and Ellery will take in this work some tiny fraction of the pride I have for them.

And finally, without my wife, Sharon, neither this nor anything else would have been possible.

About the Author

Terence Hawkins was raised in Fayette County, PA, a former coal hub later distinguished as the setting for the original *Night of the Living Dead* and *American Rust*. He graduated from Yale, where he was Publisher of the Yale Daily News, and received a law degree from the University of Wisconsin. In 2012 he became the founding Director of the Yale Writers' Conference, which he developed and managed through 2015. He is now the Director of the Company of Writers and Prose Editor of *Blue Mountain Review*.

His first novel, *The Rage of Achilles*, is a realistic and sometimes brutal account of the Iliad based on the theory of the bicameral mind. Tom Perrotta called it a "genuinely fresh take on a classic text." In naming it a Year's Best, Kirkus Reviews called his second, *American Neolithic*, "a towering work of speculative fiction."

He lives in Connecticut.

Past Titles

Running Wild Stories Anthology, Volume 1

Running Wild Anthology of Novellas, Volume 1

Jersey Diner by Lisa Diane Kastner

Magic Forgotten by Jack Hillman

The Kidnapped by Dwight L. Wilson

Running Wild Stories Anthology, Volume 2

Running Wild Novella Anthology, Volume 2, Part 1

Running Wild Novella Anthology, Volume 2, Part 2

Running Wild Stories Anthology, Volume 3

Running Wild's Best of 2017, AWP Special Edition

Running Wild's Best of 2018

Build Your Music Career From Scratch, Second Edition by Andrae Alexander

Writers Resist: Anthology 2018 with featured editors Sara Marchant and Kit-Bacon Gressitt

Magic Forbidden by Jack Hillman

Frontal Matter: Glue Gone Wild by Suzanne Samples

Mickey: The Giveaway Boy by Robert M. Shafer

Dark Corners by Reuben "Tihi" Hayslett

The Resistors by Dwight L. Wilson

Open My Eyes by Tommy Hahn

Legendary by Amelia Kibbie

Christine, Released by E. Burke

Upcoming Titles

Running Wild Stories Anthology, Volume 4

Running Wild Novella Anthology, Volume 4

Magpie's Return by Curtis Smith

Suicide Forrest by Sarah Sleeper

Tough Love at Mystic Bay by Elizabeth Sowden

The Faith Machine by Tone Milazzo

Recon: The Anthology by Ben White

The Self Made Girl's Guide by Aliza Dube

Sodom & Gomorrah on a Saturday Night by Christa Miller

Running Wild Press, Best of 2019

Running Wild Press publishes stories that cross genres with great stories and writing. Our team consists of:

Lisa Diane Kastner, Founder and Executive Editor
Barbara Lockwood, Editor
Cecile Sarruf, Editor
Peter A. Wright, Editor
Rebecca Dimyan, Editor
Benjamin White, Editor
Andrew DiPrinzio, Editor
Amrita Raman, Operations Manager
Lisa Montagne, Director of Education

Learn more about us and our stories at
www.runningwildpress.com

Loved this story and want more? Follow us at
www.runningwildpress.com, www.facebook/runningwildpress,
on Twitter @lisadkastner @RunWildBooks

CPSIA information can be obtained
at www.ICGtesting.com
Printed in the USA
LVHW021959180520
655843LV00004B/260